Shiladitya Niyogi is the bestselling author of *How Some Small Businesses Get Their Ducks in a Row and Grow* and *Lean Customer Engagement,* both published by SAGE Publications across the US, UK, and India. Acclaimed for his ability to turn real-world insights into compelling narratives, his books climbed into Amazon's Top 100 Business Bestsellers and drew praise from thought leaders around the globe. He has shared his insights on *School of Startups Radio, Indian Management Magazine,* and through his own podcast, where he interviewed bold entrepreneurs carving their path through uncertainty.

But behind the strategist's mind lies a lifelong seeker of deeper truths.

Since his college days, Shiladitya has explored the hidden dimensions of the mind—lucid dreaming, out-of-body experiences, and spiritual consciousness. His journey has taken him from silent corners of academia to intimate dialogues with spiritual circles in Los Angeles and Chicago.

Now, for the first time, he brings those obsessions to life through fiction—blurring the line between what's real and what's beyond. This is more than a story. It's a descent into the unknown, shaped by a mind that's walked the edge of logic and mystery.

ADVANCE PRAISE FOR THE BOOK

'*Run, Dad, Run* is a compelling, genre-defying thriller that masterfully blends science, the supernatural, and emotional family ties. Shil Niyogi's storytelling is cinematic, emotionally resonant, and deeply thought-provoking. As a fellow author who has explored trauma, truth, and resilience through lived experience, I found this narrative both haunting and powerful. It pulls you in with its gripping pace and leaves you questioning the very nature of memory, identity, and what it means to truly know the ones we love. An extraordinary debut that deserves wide recognition.' – Sagarika Chakraborty, author of *The Journey of a Mother* (adapted into the National Award-winning film *Mrs Chatterjee vs Norway*)

'An edge-of-the-seat ride that brings together multiple worlds of intrigue, suspense and thrills.' – Anirban Bhattacharyya, bestselling author and creator of *Savdhaan India*

'Shil Niyogi makes a confident debut with *Run, Dad, Run*. ... The characters have been meticulously created and well etched out, making the readers resonate with them and be a part of their quest. With an instantly engaging and unique plot and a highly descriptive writing style, *Run, Dad, Run* is a must-read.' – *The Times of India*

'Shil Niyogi's debut sci-fi thriller packs a punch. Unlike anything you've read lately, *Run, Dad, Run* pulls you in with its gripping storyline and a narrative rich in depth and nuance. Not only is the central plot engaging, but the author excels in creating several layers within it ... the book engages the reader from its inception with themes of time travel and teleportation intermingled with thrilling conspiracies and intense family relations. Niyogi displays a flair for writing by creating a taut book with terrific characterizations, making him an author to definitely watch out for!' – *Hindustan Times*

RUN DAD RUN

SHIL NIYOGI

Om Books International

First published in 2025

Om Books International

Corporate & Editorial Office
A-12, Sector 64, Noida 201 301
Uttar Pradesh, India
Phone: +91 120 477 4100
Email: editorial@ombooks.com
Website: www.ombooksinternational.com

Sales Office
107, Ansari Road, Darya Ganj,
New Delhi 110 002, India
Phone: +91 11 4000 9000
Email: sales@ombooks.com
Website: www.ombooks.com

ISBN: 978-93-6395-267-6

Printed in India

10 9 8 7 6 5 4 3 2 1

I dedicate this book to my very beautiful and creative wife, Aindrila Gupta, who made me believe in my strengths and whose stories found a home within these pages.

Prologue

New Delhi. December 25, 1999. Six days to Y2K.

"This is really urgent."

"Can we start next month?"

"We need you here in the next couple of days."

Anurag frowned, staring at the unusually large screen bearing the flight plans. His employer had secured him a seat on the only plane to Chicago. Today of all days.

"The timing is bad," Anurag said into the phone, watching a couple and their six kids stroll to the exit. "My family is on their way back from Calcutta now."

"I know, I know. Just this last time, buddy."

"I'm sorry James—."

"Thanks a lot. Merry Christmas—"

"James, it's not possible—"

The line was dead.

Damn it.

Anurag stood, torn amidst the pool of humans flooding the cool yet expensively decorated airport waiting hall. Red, white, and green plastered every corner, spilling the spirit of Christmas, yet Anurag could only stand in confused awe. How on earth had he come this far?

Working for a finance technology, or what his co-workers referred to as "fintech", department of a luxury company came with its set of commitments. The year 2000 would begin with a string of problems related to financial data management, particularly transactions that lacked a mention of the century. Early programmers had not foreseen that failing to depict the 19 in 1950 could pose a problem for computing beyond the 20th century. It was similar to how one makes local calls without the area code; the reference to a year had been made with two digits instead of four.

Anurag had been to the US quite a few times to deal with these issues when they happened, and he knew his way around downtown Chicago. His business visa allowed him to enter the US multiple times whenever his employer needed his expertise in solving rare problems. Now, folktales were going around, speculations about how transportation and utilities would immensely fail on the first day of the new millennium and how the world would become a zombie land of looters pillaging through the retail establishments. And today of all days, a single phone call from his employers would ruin his less ambitious plans for New Year's Eve.

His phone buzzed. He didn't have to check the caller ID to know who it was. His ringtone, a song from his least favorite musician, had been customized intentionally.

"Hello." He said, his heart skipping slightly as he heard that voice.

"Everyone is waiting. We'll need some help with the rest of the family presents."

"Sumati, I..."

"Is everything okay? Hold on, it's noisy here..." the caller said. Anurag could hear movement in the background and the sound of children yelling. What a shame he would miss it all this Christmas.

"Okay, it's quiet here. You were saying?"

"I can't make it."

The line went silent. For a moment, Anurag thought he heard her click her tongue. There was a sigh on the other end, then Sumati's voice again.

"Why do you do this?"

"It's important work, very important work."

"More important than your family?"

"Stop this, please, Sumati. You know how badly I wish I could be with my children right now."

He heard her sniff. Someone was asking her what was going on. It was Karan. His heartbeat tripled.

"Sumati?"

"I'm…I'm here."

"Please, understand."

The line was silent, punctuated only by Sumati's ragged breath.

"What do I tell the children?" she asked, her tone suddenly lenient and serious.

"Tell them I'm coming. I'll call them first thing when I reach the office—"

"I will not lie to my children."

"It's Christmas, Sumati. Don't ruin it for the kids."

"You already ruined it the moment you took this job that steals you from your family."

"I can't do this now; I have to go. Tell the kids I…hello? Hello?"

His screen was blank when he checked his phone. A flat battery. What a stupid phone, Anurag cursed. Fuming, he pushed through the queue.

Sumati and their three children, Karan, Abhi, and Chandra were visiting relatives in Calcutta (now Kolkata) for Christmas. Anurag had been with them just hours ago, but he had a few things to wrap up here in Delhi. The damned flight delays. For some reason, his flight took longer due to maintenance problems, and his family had reached Delhi ahead of him.

What made it worse was James and his manipulative games. Now, Anurag and his family had to deal with a problem caused by a different generation. The problem in Chicago was unavoidable. Call it contractual obligations. If he ever worked elsewhere, he would consider how employee-friendly the company was, at least from a family perspective. He would have to add 'heavy family time' in his 'criteria for hire' at any future job in the US.

This wasn't the first time he had missed a family function over work. One time, Sumati had urged him to update his resume and look for a job that wouldn't sap him of family life. She had mentioned how the kids complained he was hardly home, how they doubted he even cared.

Statements like that stung Anurag. Even his last conversation with his younger son, Abhi hadn't gone well. The boy had done something wrong, and instead of correcting him as any loving father would, Anurag had snapped, scolding him for watching TV. He stopped himself from blowing the incident out of proportion.

He should go home. He really should. He desperately wanted to. But he couldn't.

It was funny. Just a week ago, he had sworn to a resolution. Though never one to voice his change of heart, he had decided to make more time for his family. And yet, here he was, breaking that promise.

Still, Anurag managed to grin.

On the brighter side though, he was going to see Jenny again.

Jenny was James's assistant, a young pre-med undergrad from the University of Chicago. Her highly inquisitive nature stood out. Her networking took her places, and in one of such places, they had met. Anurag, now at that fearless middle age where charm was an asset, Anurag immediately aligned himself with the wavelengths of outspokenness and the very strong "alpha" personality in Jenny.

His interests were broad, something Jenny had noticed early on. His spectrum of 'likes' ranged from English poets and travel journalism to running supply chains in manufacturing plants and medical device innovations.

As Anurag boarded the Air India flight, he found himself drawing parallels between Jenny and Sumati—and realizing that Y2K might be the least of the problems that needed fixing. The balance sheet of his life had long lost its equilibrium; he could no longer distinguish between liabilities and assets.

As the plane took off, he watched the familiar landmarks of Old Delhi shrink below him. The roads were beautifully illuminated, dots of light embellishing the ordinary yet enriching life of the city.

Strapping his seatbelt, Anurag had no idea this would be the last time he saw India.

Chapter 1

Twenty Years Later. New Delhi. December 22, 2019. Just before the Corona virus hit the world.

It wasn't going to stop raining.

The window blinds were shut, and droplets of water burst into silvery streaks against the crystal-clear panes. Abhi's gaze was fixed on the black Mercedes that had just pulled up in front of the old family house. There was no reason to panic, yet an uneasy sensation hijacked his mind. He watched as a man and a woman in a saree stepped out of the car and walked toward the front door.

"Abhi!" The woman wrapped her arms around him.

"Hey, someone's soaked," Abhi said.

"Oh, I'm sorry."

"It's all right, Priya. It's been a while..."

"Yes," the woman in the orange saree chortled. This was Priya. Her hair resembled that of a cabaret dancer from a Bollywood number in the 1980s. There was an Indian word for such a hairdo, but Abhi gave up trying to recall it as the door clicked open, ushering in a sturdy man.

His face was sharp and round, accentuated by dense eyebrows, piercing eyes, and curly hair peppered with gray—more a testament to a robustly industrious life than to age. The man grinned complacently, walking past them.

"Pleasure to see you too," Abhi muttered as Priya accompanied the new arrival to the window. "Hey, I told you this saree would look great on you!"

Before Priya could respond, a raucous squeal rang through the house.

"He's back! My Karan is back!"

Abhi watched as the woman smothered Karan in an embrace, fighting the urge to roll his eyes. The once-silent family house now buzzed with excitement, treating Karan's return like that of a long-lost prodigal son. The irony was that the true prodigal son was right here, playing the phantom in the background. Yet Abhi wasn't surprised. After years of witnessing the same overhyped jubilation for Karan, he could only wonder if Karan had started to find it just as tiresome. Or maybe she simply preferred Karan. Priya tapped his shoulder, still giggling.

"Don't worry, you'll get this embrace too, once he's married."

"As if I care."

By seven o'clock, the table was brimming with dishes and faces long unseen. Young nephews, relatives, and long-standing neighbors perched around it, waiting for Sumati's arrival before they could devour the shimmering dishes—each bursting with colors and aromas never sampled before. The main course was Sumati's old family recipe. It had been a while since all three of her children had visited Delhi at the same time.

It was a worthy occasion, and she had deliberately taken her time before appearing, letting the sea of guests battle their hunger a little longer. Abhi observed it all from the corner where he stood, his mind spinning as he kept questioning what had brought him here, to this moment.

His mother's laughter rang through the dining room, mingling with the clatter of ceramics and cutlery. Then, she turned to her firstborn:

"So, when's the wedding, then?"

Karan sputtered, spraying some of the wine he was sipping. When he looked up, a thousand eyes glared at him—except Abhi's.

"Well, we were—"

"We're still dreaming about it, Mum. We thought maybe the end of the year," Priya interjected, dabbing her fiancé's mouth. "Isn't that right, my love?"

"Umm, yes, yes," Karan said, a vague grin slipping from his lips.

"Awesome." Sumati clapped. "That's great. It's a romantic time to get married. You see, your dad and I also took some time deciding."

"Oh, really, huh?" Priya asked, exchanging glances with Abhi and Karan.

"Yes, yes. Your father and I decided to go to a peaceful spot and..."

"Exotic," a teenage nephew chimed in, earning a wave of disapproving glares.

"We were going to get married in Paris..." Sumati's voice trailed off.

"But his family didn't think it was worth getting married outside Delhi, not to mention the financial pressure after the royal ceremony," Abhi finally spoke, pouring himself a glass over his pristine dish.

"True—weddings can be very costly these days," Priya said.

"That's the reality. Mom, am I wrong about that?"

Karan had been quiet about the wedding since then. He watched as his brother stabbed at the meat with intense disinterest.

"So, Abhi, how's work?" Karan asked.

"Cleaning all the sh** that others leave."

"I heard corporations have started layoffs—anyone you know?"

"I'm good."

"Do you—"

"It's getting hot in here," Abhi cut in. "I'm going outside to confiscate some fresh air."

"Don't try to break anything," Sumati said.

"I'll think about it... not like there's anything worth breaking."

And with that, Abhi was gone.

"I told him to get a better career, to find a girlfriend. But no, Abhi insists on holding onto that exhausting job."

"I think he's the owner's right hand," Karan said, correcting his mother, who never really understood what the job entailed. Originally, however, Karan had assumed it was just an ambiguous title—one that disguised how much Abhi's employer overworked him. He watched as his mother's mouth fell open.

"What in Heaven's name is this? Priya, are you trying to get your best friend to marry him?"

Priya was laughing. Karan couldn't tell if his mother was serious.

"You see, it depends. But if he ran his own business like his brother, then 'totally.' Karan has a personal secretary, and hundreds of people report to him. But Abhi? He's just a 'yes boy' to an American in a jacket and torn-off jeans."

Karan chuckled at the last bit. Priya elbowed him.

"It's terrible," Sumati continued. "What kind of legacy are we leaving for Chandra?"

"What did I do now?" came a voice from the entrance.

"My goodness, Chandra!"

"Priya!"

The two women rushed toward each other.

"Girl, it's been a while! When did you guys get here?"

"Just yesterday. Karan thought we should go sightseeing before today..."

"That was your idea," Karan interjected from the table.

Chandra giggled.

"And who is this young man?" Priya glanced at the gentleman standing behind Chandra.

"This," Chandra's cheeks flushed crimson, "is Pierre. Pierre, this is my sister-in-law-to-be."

"Pleased to meet you." Priya shook hands with the man, who bowed.

"My pleasure," he said, his voice thick with a French accent.

Chandra introduced Pierre to everyone—except Sumati. Her mother already knew Pierre, and she had never hidden her displeasure toward the Frenchman. The conversation around the table grew tense as Sumati turned to Pierre with a barrage of questions.

"So, are both your parents French, or is one from Africa?" came the first borderline racist remark.

"Oh, Mum!"

Sumati ignored her daughter, her steel-like eyes drilling a hole through Pierre's thick-framed glasses.

"If you marry my daughter, will you allow her to keep practicing her Indian traditions and be proud of her origins?"

The elders at the table nodded in agreement, while Chandra seethed at Sumati.

"Shandra, eet'z alryt. I'm a Frenchman. My parents, French."

"You've got a house?"

"Aaah, Mom!"

Pierre's cheeks burned, his mouth stretching into an uncomfortable grin.

"I… I rent an apartment."

"I told you all…" Sumati asserted, her eyes sweeping across the table.

"But I already own a home. Outside Europe."

Sumati moved back to her seat. She opened her mouth to speak, but Pierre was quicker.

"Ummmm, where's my friend, Abhi?"

* * *

Somewhere in the upper rooms, Abhi stared at an old family photo. Five of them were in the frame—Karan, Abhi, Sumati, Chandra, and their father. The picture was taken on his ninth birthday, the same day as Maghotsava. Karan was eleven at the time, while Chandra was set to turn five the following month. All their birth months were close, which was probably why they had always been inseparable. Karan had his arms wrapped around the newly turned nine-year-old.

Every year, around the time India celebrated Republic Day, Anurag would slip into his philosophical side, inviting younger minds to ask him about life, death, and everything in between. In the Roy household, that day had a name—Maghotsava.

Where did we lose those days?

Abhi grinned at the photo. At least they had been close. They were. In the frame, their father's hands rested on Abhi's shoulders, his sparkling eyes locked onto the camera, frozen in time. Their mother beamed with joy.

As he glanced back, Abhi struggled to piece together concrete memories of his father. He had never been home—always a terribly busy man, his presence as rare as the lost currencies of demonetization. One last time, Abhi wished he could see him. Since his disappearance twenty years ago, doubts had taken root in Abhi's mind, tangled in the already conflicted debate surrounding his unusual absence.

I'm still furious at you, old man.

His gaze fell on his father's notebook—the one filled with reflections on spirituality, faith, and key takeaways from scientific conferences.

* * *

Abhi heard voices downstairs. He recognized the high-pitched tone, like a streak of bright light in the middle of dim lamps. Chandra had arrived.

At the last moment, he stared at the photo, tapping the floor. If only he had Chandra's powers. But then again, what would he do? What would he even mean to his father if he could see him again? Whatever had caused his father's disappearance, Abhi wasn't sure he wanted to unravel the mystery. Would the old man have even wanted to see him?

Now there was another question to worry about. His relationship with his father had never been pleasant. Unfatherly phrases echoed in the back of his mind, burning like coal—words that lingered even after his father disappeared forever. Abhi smiled, thinking of how fortunate Chandra was. She had a talent that allowed her to see their father whenever she wanted.

Anurag Roy had always been supportive of Chandra and Karan. And by talent, Abhi didn't mean outstanding math scores or musical ability.

Superhuman powers, man. That's what he meant. His siblings had them.

And he didn't.

Abhi's phone rang. He stared at his old smartphone, muted it, and tucked it back into his pocket before strolling to the open balcony that framed the magnificent Greater Kailash landscape of Delhi. It was a lovely sight. He had gazed at the same view as he outgrew many sizes of shoes, yet he never tired of it—the rows of homes, the zigzagging streets, the scent of February rain on the roof terraces—

His phone rang again.

Abhi didn't bother checking. It was the same caller. He ran a hand through his hair, wiped his forehead, and left his hair in a chaotic mess. His mind was just as tangled. He was in trouble. Big trouble.

He knew who was calling. The same private number had been ringing all week. Abhi had assumed they would give up. Who was he kidding? Ever since he got tangled with a supplier in the cutthroat world of cocaine and street violence, he never imagined things could go south so fast.

He had made one mistake—befriending a heroin dealer. Why they were mates was a complicated story he avoided thinking about; it gave him heartache. Yeah, it involved a tragic love tale.

Anyway, he had borrowed money from one of his dealer's clients and refused to pay it back. He figured their tight friendship would make it disappear. But that kind of thinking, if left unchecked, could get you buried alive.

That is, if you were lucky.

Abhi shook off the gruesome thought, blowing a smoke ring and letting it drift until it disappeared into the thick, gray, gloomy atmosphere. He heard footsteps. Abhi glanced upward but resisted the temptation to hide the smoke and gave it up.

"There you are, big brother." Chandra was all smiles.

"When are you going to quit blowing smoke everywhere?" she asked, still laughing. Her brother liked to conceal it out of reverence for their parents and the good Indian values they had instilled.

"Good God," she said. "You're lean. What have you been eating?"

"And your head looks thinner," Abhi retorted. "Tell me, French food isn't exhausting your reasoning ability right now, Chandra, right?"

Chandra struck him on the back of his shoulder.

"Aooh."

"Sorry. Okay, I'm not sorry," Chandra said. "There's someone I want you to meet, though."

Abhi noticed the gentleman who had been hidden in the darkness all this while.

"No way! Did he come with you?" Abhi's smile grew as they walked toward the Frenchman. Like old friends, they exchanged smiles. Abhi turned to Chandra.

"Haha, wow," he grinned. "Tell me, how did it go with Mother?"

* * *

Karan, Chandra, and Abhi had been preparing for quite a while to surprise their mother, Sumati, with a Christmas visit to Delhi. It was decided that they would do so during a less busy season—the last couple of weeks of the year. However, they all had to be in Chicago right around Christmas, as they had scheduled a New Year's party at the Ritz-Carlton in downtown Chicago.

Chapter 2

New Delhi, December 23, 2019

Abhi hung upside down.

Spending the night at the family house, he headed to the office-assigned hotel at dawn. He had a plane to catch later that night and kept experiencing an awful migraine. It had to be the beverages he had with the French. Over the past few months, he and Pierre had spoken a few times on the phone. Last night was the first time they had met in person. Pierre thought highly of Abhi. "He is out-of-this-world smart," he had said to Chandra once, and Chandra had related that to Abhi after adding other strong adjectives and prodigious nouns. Abhi merely nodded at the comments, and last night, when he had seen the Frenchman, he had felt like it was not the first time.

They had a little too much to drink that night and also had an opportunity to exchange photos of some old albums and debate them while looking at the stars for the rest of the night.

Two young men, Abhi thought, looking at the ceiling as he hung upside down, his legs far apart on the inversion bar. He had taken up this new inversion activity when his physiotherapist showed him the comfort it brought to the body—particularly the backbone. It was meditative as well. However, Abhi was distracted by the memory of how he had spent last night.

The landline was buzzing.

Abhi remained in that pose. Only one person would know where he was lodged right now.

The voicemail came in, and Abhi could hear Lewis' voice.

"Abhi, are you in there? I know you're out there. Pick up your cell. Pick it up, darn it!"

Abhi stayed locked in that position, his eyes stuck to the ceiling as he listened to his boss rant, waiting for him to get to the point.

"I don't care if you miss your flight tonight—you better not drop in late tomorrow. You're too close to being terminated, you hear me? You're running out of excuses, Abhi."

Some moments of silence passed, and Lewis' voice became smooth now.

"When you get this, make sure you dial Mulligan. He wants your assistance with accounting."

The line dropped.

* * *

The clock struck seven that night in Chicago when a rotund Indian accountant interrupted his daily ritual of glancing through his business papers. It was his practice to drop by the bar every night to run over the paperwork planned for the next day.

He saw a pretty lady step in. She was a client at the pub, or at least she seemed like one. He had seen her there on the few nights she had visited. She had shown him all the telltale signs that she was into him.

As she ambled her way to where he was sitting, chatting with the bartender, he pretended to be looking through his documents, his square glasses dangling at the side of his nose.

"Hello there, Mr. Money," said the lady as she sank into a chair a few feet away.

He wasn't turning to see her. He should have noticed her in a space packed with thousands of people. Her perfume gave her away very quickly. It was distinct, with a trace of orange and a subtle hint of cinnamon and apple cider. It was a seductive scent.

She was wearing the same floral skirt she had worn the first day they spoke. While it had been a short-lived discussion, both had an enjoyable time. He found her desirable. There was a sense of purity, yet a rebellious feel to her mannerisms. That combination had such a great impact on him that it made him want to get closer to her… and perhaps even explore a relationship.

"Hi, Nina," he said, moving his eyes from the pile of documents that had lost his interest the moment he felt her presence.

"It seems we've got a lot of paperwork to sort through today." She sat on the bar counter, tilting her head playfully.

For the first time, he glanced at her—her shiny cherry lipstick, her cleavage strategically positioned between her choker and necklace. He had to change his lenses, making a deliberate decision not to be distracted.

"Are you listening to me?"

"Sorry," he said, blinking as he pulled his thighs close.

"I said you never had to tell me what it was that you did for a living. You come here every day..."

"Every day, huh?"

She nodded. "Each day, sir. Not a day goes by without me seeing you reading through these filthy old parchments."

"I didn't know I was being tracked," he said, his eyes drifting back to her necklace.

"You didn't answer the question, sir," she said, leaning forward.

"Well... I... I work for a small accounting firm." He choked as the words rolled off his tongue. Realizing he had offered a bit too much, he grinned nervously, took a shot from his bottle, and turned to her with a shrug. "It depends on how you see it," he added, lifting a seductive brow.

"Well, do you really want to know what I know?"

"I'm dying to hear that."

"I'm wondering," she said, "are we going to stand here, Mr. Borda, or are we heading to another bar—or even getting a room?"

Minutes later, Borda and Nina forced open the hotel door, clasping at each other's clothing as they basked in the joy of their bodies—falling onto the sofa, the floor, the bed, and back to the floor. Borda hesitated with his belt, laughing awkwardly as she stood there, waiting.

"What is it?" he said, noticing she had stopped, a glint of darkness in her pupils. "What the hell's wrong?"

She was walking backward. Borda caught her, pulling at her clothing. In that instant, a bolt of pain pierced the base of his skull. He tumbled, his forehead slamming into Nina. The next thing he knew, someone was pulling his hair. He tripped, his jeans tangled around his feet. He barely had time to register the burning pain coursing through his bloodstream before something icy brushed against his forehead.

He screamed when he saw the handgun.

A woman stood behind him, pistol aimed at his skull. Wait—his frown deepened as the nightmare unfolded further. The face staring back at him was another Nina. Her hair was thinner. She was wearing a black leather dress.

"Why is that gun pointing at me?" he asked.

"Fair question," said the woman, pointing the gun.

When he turned, his eyes remained wide. Standing behind him, gun aimed at his chest was Tina—Nina's twin sister—her lips smeared from their violent kissing.

"So, wait, who was with me this whole time... I'm confused..." Borda thought cracking a joke might diffuse the situation.

"Mr. Borda," one of them said, pushing the pistol further into his chest, "you need to make a call."

* * *

Abhi rose, scratching the back of his head as he picked up the phone and pressed the message button. The screen read: *Speed-dialing Mulligan, Welling.*

As he waited for the connection, Abhi wondered how an idiot like Lewis had managed to obtain a high office in the organization. If the world was filled with people like Lewis, he might as well give up hope of career progression entirely.

"Mulligan," the line announced.

"Yes, hi, Mulligan, this is Abhi..."

"Uhun, huh?"

"The boss said to call. He mentioned you needed some help."

"There's nothing here, boy!"

The call ended.

Abhi stood there for a moment, taking stock of the chaos he had to endure with these dimwits. He disconnected the phone—then it rang again.

The caller ID read: *Mulligan and Shekhar.*

Click.

"Hello?"

"Hey," a voice blared on the line. "This is Shekhar... Borda..."

Abhi raised an eyebrow, trying to recognize the caller's voice. This was the first time he had spoken to Mulligan's partner.

"Yeah... was trying to see if there was something I could help you with. Lewis asked me to call—"

"Yes, Mulligan just texted me."

Abhi furrowed his brow. The man on the line sounded nervous, as if under some kind of tension.

"O—all right."

"You're already at the hotel, right?"

"Of… course…" Abhi said, his gut tightening. Something felt off, but he couldn't quite place it. Not yet.

"So, we need a favor, Abhi. We've been waiting for some files from Shah and Patel Chartered Accountants—our external auditors in Delhi. They were supposed to ship them this Thursday, but they had some power issues."

"Can't they just email them or upload them to a secure server?" Abhi asked.

"Well, since you're already there, we were hoping you could pick up the physical files."

"I don't know, Borda." Abhi rubbed his neck. "I've got a couple of errands to run. I might miss my flight."

"It shouldn't take more than an hour—you can stop by on your way to the airport."

"Tonight, huh?" Abhi massaged his temple.

"Is that cool?"

Abhi hesitated. This was the part he hated most. Lewis had a habit of making him run errands outside his job description. But who could he complain to? Abhi sighed and found his voice.

"Where's the location?"

"I'll text you the address. I'll let them know in case you're running late."

Abhi sank into the chair. "And remember, this is just a one-time favor."

"Will do. I've emailed the office that you're coming."

"Okay."

"Are you at the Imperial?"

"Yes, I was with my family earlier this week."

"Yeah, just checking. Well, thanks a lot, man. I owe you."

Abhi massaged his temple. His head was pounding. Something felt off—really off. But he couldn't quite place it. Borda was a stark contrast to Mulligan and Lewis. There was humility in his request.

* * *

Abhi stared out the cab window, his gaze shifting between Borda's text and the dilapidated Welling Trade building. He fiddled with his phone. The signage was missing bulbs in the "W" of "Welling" and even the "T," making it easy to overlook the place if one was searching by name rather than building number. Had he gotten the address wrong? The building hardly looked corporate—it resembled a discarded piece of furniture forcefully wedged into a prime property. If anything, it looked like a tech startup thriving off illegitimate revenues from companies growing at a similar exponential speed.

"Shitty maintenance," Abhi thought.

He dialed Borda's number and was met with static, followed by an answering machine instructing him to leave a message. He hung up, a faint headache creeping in. Four calls now—same response.

Earlier, Borda had sent two messages. The first was the address. The second had been brief: *Told the folks you're on your way - safe travels.*

Abhi had expected a call from Lewis. Normally, when dealing with finances or accounting, Lewis—ever the micromanager—would drop a note. But not today. Abhi debated calling him, knowing he risked being *blasted* for asking too many *simple* questions and interrupting *happy hour.* He tried a few times, only to hear that the recipient was on another call.

Before calling Uber, Abhi had packed his briefcase. He

searched his back pocket for his wallet, then checked his carry-on bag for his passport and flight tickets.

It was going to be a long night.

"I cannot wait for more than 15 minutes—personal reasons."

"What?" Abhi frowned at the driver from the back seat, eyebrows raised. He slammed the door shut, glancing at his watch as he paid and dismissed the Uber driver.

It was 7:45 p.m. All employees would have gone home except the one handing over the package.

He planned to wrap things up by 8:30 p.m., then head to the airport reception for a power nap before his flight. With that in mind, he ambled through the winding entrance of Welling Trade, the doors slamming shut like hell's trapdoor.

Inside, it was dark, with sharp beams of streetlights piercing through holes in the walls. The ground floor was empty—just vacant space. Abhi coughed as the musty air hit him, his gaze sweeping over the barren interior.

In the corner, a flight of stairs led upward. He headed that way, pinching his nose as he climbed. The stench of mold was suffocating, as if a flood had once swept through and no one had bothered with cleanup. He made a conscious effort not to touch the walls—moss-covered and crumbling, slowly being consumed by cracks and bio-organisms.

After several flights, Abhi stepped into a well-lit corridor. Most offices were empty, untouched for what seemed like a long time. Sweat soaked his shirt. The air here was marginally cleaner.

He trudged forward until he reached a small office—Suite 333.

Inside, the room was nearly barren. A low table, a discolored chair with a bad leg, and a metal shelf filled with cartons. No files. No documents.

Seemed like not a soul had been here in years.

Abhi's stomach growled. Surreal. Was this a prank? Or the wrong address? His eyes scanned the corridor—it looked like a scene ripped straight from a horror movie.

Two picture frames hung on the wall, asymmetrical and poorly placed. One held a portrait of a man with a thick mustache—his eyes torn out of the photo. The other frame was empty, its glass cover shattered.

Creeeakkk.

Abhi turned sharply, nearly stumbling in fear. The door behind him was open.

It's just a door.

Air rushed through a window with iron bars, but that didn't stop the sweat pooling on his forehead. He wiped it away and made his way back to the staircase.

As he hurried, the lights flickered.

He stopped and looked back. "Hello… is anyone there?"

The only response was his own voice echoing off the walls, bouncing back at him. There was no one there—just furniture and piles of cardboard. Not a soul to offer him a seat or a cup of coffee. Just a hollow building. A soulless shell.

Was this some kind of joke Borda played? Was that even Borda he had spoken to? And why had Mulligan gotten him to do this job?

His phone rang.

Abhi's breath caught as he looked at the caller ID. The same private number.

Panic surged through him. He bolted down the stairs, misstepping and twisting his knee in the process. He groaned in pain as he reached the ground floor.

Something was wrong.

The entrance.

His gut screamed, *"No, no, no!"*

He ran to the steel doors and grabbed the iron bars, shaking them violently. They didn't budge.

"Not now. God, no..." he muttered, shrugging off his jacket, his muscles tensing as he pulled at the bars again with all his strength.

His phone rang.

Sweat dripped down his temple as he reached for the auto *I'm busy now* text message. His thumb trembled over the screen.

Instead, he hit the call-receive icon.

"Welcome to Accounting Unlimited—directing your call. Please wait a moment... Would you like to listen to our offers while you wait? Press one to listen..."

Abhi's irritation spiked. An automated message? Now?

"Please note, offers will self-delete in twenty seconds."

What?

His brows furrowed as he ran a hand through his hair, massaging his temple. What was this message even asking him to do?

"Whatever," he muttered and pressed one.

* * *

The air was dense with the smell of mold, and the floor was littered with pieces of office essentials that had grown cobwebs over the years. The space was empty except for his breathlessness, a phone stuck to his ear, his back against the doors like a prisoner sentenced to an electric chair.

Abhi waited as the line went silent for a moment. An Indian ringtone played in the background. The line clicked, and he sensed that someone had picked up.

"If you're listening to this..." the caller said, his sentences harsh and breathless, "...you're in grave danger."

Chills ran down Abhi's spine. "Who… who is this?"

"You are probably disturbed right now. You're wondering who this is and why I have called," the voice said. It almost sounded like Abhi's own voice. "My identity is unimportant. Right now, you must know that you're in grave danger—"

"OK, OK, what are you—"

"You have something they want, something they'll stop at nothing to get… You must flee, Abhi. I am on your side. Flee. They—"

"What're you talking about…"

"...have eyes everywhere. You must run, Abhi."

"Hold on, are you listening to what I'm saying..."

But the line continued as though the caller hadn't understood a word he said. Then, the message stopped by itself—it was pre-recorded.

"...they are coming for me—argggh!"

Silence. The message was done. The lights in the corridor began to flicker.

Abhi broke into a frenzy, running up the stairs, then rushing back down after realizing he had no idea where they led. No more wrong turns—he needed to get out of this building and to the airport.

His bad knee was killing him, but something much bigger was about to happen.

Why him?

The lights in the office kept fluctuating as he ran. He halted; his mouth dry as his gaze shot toward the wall with the pictures.

He saw things. No, he told himself, shaking his head. He was going nuts. The picture frames… the photo frames…

They were… gone. Was it all false… a bad dream?

Abhi fled desperately, searching anywhere—everywhere—for an escape. He took a deep breath, his mind repeating the same words: a way out.

His eyes locked onto a strange-looking door, where bits of sunlight leaked through holes at the joints. He hurled himself at it—only to land hard on his back.

This is jarred.

He rammed the door again—first with his body, then with his feet—gritting his teeth as sharp pain tore through his left knee. Frustrated, he scanned the room and spotted a rust-filled metal shelf lying nearby. This is a light rack, he thought.

Gripping it tightly, he lifted it and rushed toward the door. Abhi took a deep breath, filled his lungs with air, and drove the shelf into the door.

Crack. Crack.

On the third strike, the door finally gave way. And that's when he realized—it wasn't a door at all. It was a window. And on the other side, there was no floor. No stairs.

Oh no. Damn. "Doorway to Heaven," he muttered, breathing in the fresh air. Gooseflesh prickled his skin, a wave of cold washing over him as his blood turned to ice. How had he not noticed this before? He was on the sixth floor.

Staring down, he saw the meandering path where the cab had dropped him off—impossibly far below.

I've been trapped!

He turned, heading for the stairs, when he heard it—noises. Footsteps. Abhi steadied himself, trying to keep his breathing even.

Bang!

He clamped a hand over his mouth, forcing himself into silence. Was someone shooting at him? Or was someone else being murdered?

His primal 'flight' instinct kicked in. He crawled forward, the humid air clinging to his sweat-soaked skin. He reached the curtain.

Bang!

The lights went out.

Abhi peered into the darkness, his pulse hammering in his ears. His feet wobbled. The world spun. The footsteps were closing in.

Then, a barrel emerged from the shadows. He barely had time to react.

Aaaaahhhhhhhh!

Abhi screamed. *Abhi* was freefalling.

Chapter 3

December 24, 2019; Chicago

Karan and Priya had been sleeping for 12 hours after their flight back to Chicago. When he woke up, Karan looked out at his front yard, the sun glimmering on fresh snow, as a sickening churn started in his stomach. He sensed Priya approaching.

"Good morning, my love," Priya said, embracing him and planting a kiss on his cheek.

"Morning."

"Hope you slept well?"

Karan forced a pained smile. "I got some sleep."

"So did I. Would you like a cup of coffee?"

"No, Priya, I don't want a cup of coffee," he said, leaving his fiancée by the bed. A dull, bulging pain throbbed in his skull. It wasn't his organization that worried him—he had worked to build a business that could function without his constant presence. There were always rumors: consulting firms like his were deemed unprofitable, overly dependent on independent workers. Yet, that wasn't what troubled Karan this morning. It was something else—something that had been brought up at the dining table back in Delhi.

Back in Delhi, Chandra had talked about her dissertation. It had something to do with psychoanalysis, and somehow the conversation had led to a detailed discussion about their father,

Anurag Roy, who had disappeared after a trip to Chicago some twenty years ago. Nothing of his had ever been found. The Indian Airline agency in Chicago had provided video footage—proof that Anurag had indeed gotten off the plane and boarded a taxi. The only issue was that the taxi's plate number was unclear and couldn't be identified. Investigators had reached out to the company Anurag worked for, and a representative confirmed that the last they'd heard from him was through a phone call. They said he was in Chicago to wrap up some work. Shortly after arriving, Anurag called his boss to inform them of his arrival. However, that was the last time anyone had heard from him.

After the dinner conversation, while Priya and Chandra helped their mother with the dishes, Karan had called his friend, Ross.

Ross was a private detective. He and Karan went way back to when Karan was earning his master's in artificial intelligence, while Ross was investigating a civil lawsuit against the university. Back in their school days, Karan and Ross hadn't discussed his father's disappearance in depth. However, just before Karan had boarded a plane to India, he had unexpectedly run into Ross after several years. Ross had mentioned his new enterprise and his interest in retracing Anurag's steps.

"A taxi with an obscured number plate can be tracked, Karan! Why didn't you tell me about this earlier?"

"I... I didn't realize that. The other investigators—they told us there was little we could do about it—"

"Bullshit, man!" Ross said.

Karan listened quietly. When the call ended, a dull ache began to spread through his head. Ross had raised some thought-provoking questions. The increasing influx of Indians and other job-seeking nationals to America was, perhaps, starting to unsettle some people. Karan had never considered that being an immigrant could be a problem—not with the contributions and sacrifices that generations of immigrants had made on American soil. However, Ross had explained that investigators were often overworked, making it easier to dismiss cold cases, especially those involving immigrants. It wasn't that they gave up entirely on such cases, Ross added—they just treated them with less urgency, particularly if the individuals involved were from certain countries. Moreover, investigations that weren't pursued promptly could lose their trail quickly, especially when foreign travel was involved. For once, Karan felt grateful he had bumped into Ross Loffers at the airport.

For Karan, spirituality meant understanding oneself and the purpose behind everything. Yet he also knew that goals could shift—what seemed crucial one moment could become insignificant the next. Throughout college, Karan had explored studying through dreams. While he had some success, there were still mysteries he couldn't unravel. One question that constantly plagued him was what gave people a clear sense of their goals in life and how to invest their attention in pursuits that truly mattered.

* * *

December 2017, Chicago, a throwback to two years ago right around the same time

Nobody could manage dreams the way Karan did. He knew what to dream, and there it was—like a gift that never failed. If he didn't consciously decide what to dream, his mind would automatically replay a previous one, like an in-built randomizer. Karan understood that dreams were one of the few realms beyond human control, yet he had heard of mathematicians turning to dreams to seek solutions.

As a lucid dreamer, Karan often found answers to his questions through lucid dreams. He had even connected with friends while dreaming and could occasionally see what they dreamt. Fascinated by this, he began exploring whether communication through dreams could be possible. One of his ambitions was to create an information highway through dreams—clear, bidirectional communication akin to the internet, yet far more advanced. Without the need for software, hardware, upgrades, or electricity, the idea of such a network could transform communication.

In school, Karan had shared his ideas with a close friend. At the time, he was just beginning—able to control his own dreams but still seeking deeper understanding. He had connected with groups exploring this realm, including those who believed they had extrasensory perception. Whenever he found answers, new questions emerged. When his friends suggested pursuing a utility patent and building a business around solving mysteries, Karan realized that such an endeavor would need extensive research and funding. That was when he understood he needed a viable business—a concrete source of resources that could eventually support his vision for dream-based communication. Dreaming alone wouldn't be enough, at least not then.

Alongside his persistent search for his father, Karan had also started taking an interest in the lives of his neighbors.

"Did anything fun happen this week?" Karan had just initiated what could possibly become another conversation that led to talking about dogs.

Karan and Bhavna were at the kennel club. Bhavna was a psychology major, and she confided everything in Hugo, her best friend. Hugo was a male Labrador with a certain strangeness about him. On a previous Christmas Day, when Bhavna had opened the door for the newspaper, little Hugo had been there holding it. It seemed that the *Wall Street Journal* and Santa Claus had co-planned this Christmas gift.

For Ajit Sengupta, Bhavna's father, entering the investment industry might not have been his first choice—until he met an alumnus who encouraged him to pursue the safer field of fixed-income securities. Ajit had been working in the investment industry for twenty-seven years now. Little did he know how stressful his life would become when the money of the populous was in question.

That was Christmas Eve morning, and the phones had been ringing non-stop. In the spirit of extending a helping hand to his family, Hugo made every effort to alert the family members of the ringing phones.

Dealing with people's opinions about him came naturally to Hugo. He had been a difficult trainee at his school and had been counseled out of almost every school he had attended. His lack of adherence to instructions and discipline seemed incorrigible.

"He never fetches the ball and does not listen to me, Bhavna," the last Russian trainer had said a year ago. Bhavna agreed that Hugo was a dogmatic dog who followed only what he knew best.

"Hugo and I had a blast shopping. Right, Hugo?" Bhavna informed Karan.

Karan had become interested in Bhavna when he saw her at a Bengali Association of Greater Chicago community event in a sari. He was struck by her traditional Indian look—bangles, mehndi (temporary tattoo-like Indian body art using a plant-based paste), and the Bollywood hairdo. Bhavna's curly hair framing her chiselled face made her stand out in any crowd. She had a curvy, feminine figure and knew how to maintain her beauty with the Indian herbal masks her mother believed would lighten her skin.

On one hand, Karan considered Bhavna a great friend, but on the other, he kept her on his list of potential wives. He kept this preoccupation to himself, just as he kept his search for his father a secret.

Then there was Bruno, the borrowed dog Karan used to get enrolled in the kennel club. Bruno belonged to Karan's friend, but Bhavna had mistakenly assumed that Karan was his owner when he brought Bruno to the club in his friend's absence. Karan loved that identity and continued with it, earning himself a spot in the hall of dog lovers. Over the past ten months, he hadn't taken Bruno to the club meetings, but he continued attending them alone to learn more about dog training, dietary habits, and other canine topics.

"Bruno hasn't seen Hugo in a long time."

"Yes—even Hugo has been missing him," Bhavna chuckled.

"How does it sound to have them meet at 7 p.m.? By then, I'll be done with some errands. I'm working on a white paper on advancements in the psycho-electronic industry."

Karan often found himself overexplaining when it came to Bhavna; her presence made him shy and nervous. He avoided long conversations, fearing that her depth and intellect would expose his own perceived shallowness. What if he stuttered over Democrat policies? What if she found out he knew nothing about Shakespearean literature? What if he didn't recognize popular songwriters? And what if she hated *South Park* or some stand-up comedian he admired?

Still, Karan had asked Bhavna out informally in subtle and less sophisticated ways. He had once offered to pick up her dry cleaning—and get coffee on the way. He had also asked her to attend an art exhibition. His other attempts included suggesting bowling, going to the movies, grabbing ice cream, and starting a book club at a local library.

"I'm sorry, Karan! Unfortunately, I have to be at the H4H fundraising," Bhavna replied. *Habitat for Humanity* involved volunteers like Bhavna who helped build houses for lower-income groups. She had previously spent countless hours educating wealthy donors and ensuring their contributions reached the right people.

"The weekend?" Karan asked.

"Yes, we can do the weekend."

"In that case, I would have to dress to impress."

Karan wanted to be sure that this was taken as a date and not just a casual meet-up, so he didn't wait for a response.

* * *

Shekhar was a strong advocate of logic and all things philosophical—a trait that often made him downright argumentative. Everyone called him "Borda," a variation of *Boro-dada* (older brother in Bengali), whether it was his parents, Bhavna, or even his co-workers.

Ajit and Kabita had made sure that Bhavna and her older brother, Shekhar—*or Borda*—spoke Bengali at home. Shekhar assisted his father in his entrepreneurial pursuits and had majored in accounting.

* * *

December 23, 2019, Chicago

Multiple phones were ringing. As Abhi woke up, he smelled coffee that his neighbor had brewed and left outside his door, along with a slice of pumpkin spice cake.

"Welcome back—Merry Christmas! I thought you were coming back tomorrow. Oh well!" the note read.

Abhi stood up, looking confused. He glanced out the window, and his eyes brightened. He quickly examined his body—no scratches, no gunshot wounds, no bruises. Nothing.

He checked his watch—it was 9 a.m. on December 23, 2019. The last time he had checked it was 8:30 p.m. on December 23, at the dilapidated building. What on earth had happened? How did he make the Delhi flight and wind up at his flat in Chicago? Or was it all just a long, bad dream? He massaged his head, blinking. He wasn't dreaming. He knew he wasn't. Was he dead?

When he checked his phone, he saw several text messages from his mom and brother. He immediately texted his mom, letting her know he was safe and back in Chicago, but her phone was switched off.

He tried calling Karan, who lived in Winnetka, just half an hour from downtown Chicago and close to his alma mater, Northwestern University. Karan didn't pick up, so Abhi left a long message.

Was he forgetting some package he needed from wherever he had been just an hour ago in India? His mental alarm was screaming: *You're crazy, and you're about to get fired!*

Abhi slept for what seemed like a very long time. In the psychic world it is established that Teleporters feel sleepy after teleporting and sleep for a day or more to get charged. When Abhi woke up he muttered "Did I teleport? Did I just sleep for one full day? Am I dreaming now?" Anurag had meditated about it before but had never managed to do it himself.

Chapter 4

"I don't understand."

"He called last night, I have proof—"

"Just shut up, Abhi! Just shut up!" yelled the young man in a jacket and skinny jeans. "What's the time right now... goddammit, answer me!"

"It's pretty late."

"Damn right it is... it's freaking Thursday morning, and the best lie you can come up with is that sly rant about Borda—"

"He called me, I saw—" Abhi stopped himself, gritting his teeth. "I have proof of it... right here, on my phone."

"Alright, show me," Lewis demanded.

Abhi took out his phone. It was off. That was unusual—he never turned off his phone. Not like you have a bully like Lewis as your manager. As the phone booted up, Abhi fumbled through his texts. His eyebrows shot up.

"It was... it was here..." Abhi whispered, staring at the screen. To his shock, all his calls had been deleted. No contacts, no call history, no emails, no texts. Just a few random apps—Angry Chickens, Candy Smashing, and some others he never played.

"Someone's messed up my phone... Lewis, I... I had it in here."

"I'm sure you did."

"I saw—he texted me. He said the company needed some records—"

"Keep the phone."

"He texted me," he muttered as he walked away.

* * *

"Hi, Borda here. Just leave a message, and I'll get back to—"

Beep beep.

Abhi slammed his phone on the desk. Borda had been unreachable all day. Abhi could handle insults from the higher-ups, but he couldn't stand his work reputation being tainted. He didn't mess around with his responsibilities—he guarded them with ironclad rigor. While others worked nine to five, he started at home as early as five, rarely left before eight-thirty, and often resumed on his computer back at his apartment before calling it a day.

The H-1B visa was granted to foreigners with specialized skills seeking work in the United States. Congress introduced it in 1990 to address the shortage of highly skilled workers that the domestic workforce couldn't fully supply. However, issues surrounded the H-1B program. Many companies began outsourcing jobs and entire departments to agencies relying solely on H-1B candidates because it was more cost-effective.

Abhi understood the complexities of H-1B visas and wasn't about to jeopardize everything he'd worked for. That's why, when he got a harsh reprimand that morning, he took it silently, nodded politely, and checked his schedule without complaint. He knew it would take at least twenty-five hours to make up for the wasted time today. Piles of tasks awaited him, along with a few unusually demanding clients he had to call. But that was the easy part—he still had to write extensive requirements for the new software the company was preparing to launch.

Amid it all, Abhi was still wrestling with the question of how he had ended up in the US overnight when his eyes fell on his journal. His expression crumbled.

"Oh no," he muttered, staring at the orange writing scrawled across the page. The handwriting wasn't his. Worse, the date marked on the journal was one he'd already crammed. The words read: "Call Bhavna!"

* * *

Bhavna was a woman his mom had tried to set him up with. Abhi had lofty expectations when it came to relationships. Over the past two years, he had met plenty of potential partners, all of whom had been shown the door.

Three weeks ago, his mom had asked him to put a reminder note in his journal. The first time she'd reached out in months. Abhi knew right away that he was about to negotiate what his mom called "relationship rites." She had tried to offer him a match a few months back, around Durga Puja, through a contact she had stumbled upon. "Limited edition," she liked to call it. She never failed to find potential matches, thanks to her vast network of aristocratic friends who boasted both wealth and intellectual prowess.

"And what's wrong with my friends bringing a girl for my son to marry?" Sumati had asked when he brought it up.

"The past few ones ended so well," Abhi replied, grinning.

"Abhi, you'll like her. I heard she's also into telecommunication consulting, just like you."

"Mom, I'm not in telecommunications!" Abhi said, wondering why he even bothered correcting her when she'd soon forget. "I don't think it's fair for me to go through another series of Q and A's with a girl your friends think will be a great match."

"Abhi, she is—"

"No, Mom, not today."

He could hear his mom's exhausted breath leaking over the line. "Okay... it's alright..."

"I'm sorry, Mom."

"It's okay... it's alright... I see how much you value freedom... like your father... bachelor life and all..."

Here we go again, Abhi sighed. "It's... it's not all true. I just... I..."

"Yes," Abhi finally said. "I think I like how things are right now."

"It's okay then. I need to go now."

Abhi felt bad when she got off the phone. Days later, though, he had connected with a few girls from his mother's list. Abhi had grinned—when would his mother let him be?

He went back and used his template letter to email the address his mom had texted him. Abhi began with an introduction—one he had likely sent to at least fifty people before this.

"I got your email from my parents and thought of dropping a line to you. Just to give you a quick rundown—I came to the US over a decade ago. I got my civil engineering degree in Delhi and worked in consulting here for a few years before going back to business school for my MBA in LA. I started working with a California-based startup to understand firsthand the challenges of running a business. I racked up travel points pretty fast. These days, I'm managing sales at a boutique firm in Chicago and staying local. I guess I've started liking the lifestyle—I can focus more on myself, go to the gym, cook and eat healthy, and connect and reconnect with friends. That's pretty much what I do. How about you?"

Abhi, however, decided to tweak his template this time as the existing ones were not yielding much interest.

Chapter 5

December 25, 2019, Delhi

Sumati was sweeping her husband's study again tonight. She ran her fingers over the dense books, catching dust on her fingertips. Every anniversary, she would come down to see her rival—the study, as she often called it. It was the only thing that had taken her husband from her when they were together. There, she saw a picture of Anurag with the entire family, celebrating Maghotsava.

For a long time, Sumati Roy had convinced herself that her husband, Anurag, had abandoned her for another woman. However, there was also a parallel theory—a suspicion of his cold-blooded murder. But could there really be a motive for that?

Anurag had flown to Chicago on December 25th for a series of meetings at the Willis Tower before the client went live with their financial product on December 29th. He didn't keep Sumati informed about every detail, but he used to present a weekly overview of his work. On January 1st, he had called Sumati in the morning to wish her a Happy New Year and a Happy New Millennium, but the call ended abruptly.

Anurag and Sumati had been going through a rough patch in their relationship and had even considered separation. Yet, it was Anurag who tried to keep things together. On that January 1st call, Anurag was apologetic, but a woman could be heard speaking loudly in the background. Sumati distinctly remembered the voice repeatedly saying, "Dr. X is here. Please see her immediately." Just as Anurag was speaking, the call disconnected.

Sumati didn't call him back immediately—she was still upset. That was the last time she ever spoke to him.

A day later, Sumati began calling Anurag—she must have called a thousand times. Since Anurag worked as an independent consultant, essentially serving as his own human resources department, there was no one Sumati could reach out to when she didn't hear from him for days.

James, the contract manager, was close to Anurag and considered him someone who could solve any problem. However, he had no idea of Anurag's whereabouts. He wasn't even aware that Anurag's contract had ended after January 1st. They had said their goodbyes after the successful Go Live, and James had then become absorbed in his family holiday vacation. He never reconnected with Anurag after that.

Jenny, James's assistant, had been fired a month before the Go Live for embezzling money from James. Sumati had even contacted Jenny to see if Anurag had reached out to her, but she hadn't heard from him either.

With the help of family and friends in the US, Sumati hired detectives to find Anurag. The investigators worked tirelessly, but no closure came. After a few months, the leads went cold. The only trace left behind was Anurag's metal ring, found at a hotel he had stayed at. It had his name, "Anurag," engraved on it.

There were so many unanswered questions—so many things Anurag had left unresolved. How would she raise their children alone? Where would she live? How would she earn a livelihood? Even when they had briefly considered separation, they hadn't truly thought through the logistics.

For a long time, Sumati had believed that Anurag was having an affair. She had seen text messages on his phone that fueled her suspicions, convincing her that he was involved with someone else. Separation seemed like the only remedy for the betrayal and deception. Yet, Anurag's sudden disappearance was both shocking and completely unexpected. Despite their differences, Sumati still wished for his well-being.

However, Anurag's aunt had hinted at Sumati's involvement in his disappearance, casting a shadow of suspicion over her. For three long years, the Roy family remained in shock, but as time passed, everyone began focusing on their own lives. Sumati had three children to raise, and it became her priority to ensure they got into good schools, built strong values, respected their elders, secured well-paying jobs, and established themselves as experts in their chosen fields.

* * *

Every year, around the last week of January, Anurag would share his spiritual side with the children, discussing divine subjects and encouraging them to ask questions about life and death. There was a special day in the Roy household for this—Maghotsava. During these moments, he would explain verses from the holy Indian text, the Upanishads.

"Brahma Kripahi Kevalam," he would say in his rich, baritone voice that sounded like mahogany ear candy, "stands for the universal oneness of God."

Anurag's father was a renowned historian and a devout Brahmo, and the training Anurag had received during his school days allowed him to pass this knowledge on to his children. The kids learned about the principles of Brahmo Samaj, a social movement started by the philanthropist Raja Ram Mohan Roy in the 19th century as part of the Bengal Renaissance. Anurag also ensured that they grasped the fundamental tenets of other faiths.

He often explained how Indian society had been plagued by social evils like the caste system, idol worship, widow discrimination, and other corrupt practices rooted in the misinterpretation of Hindu scriptures by priests and clergy. However, Raja Ram Mohan Roy and his followers rejected these norms prevalent in pre-renaissance Bengal. The movement gathered momentum, attracting the rich and influential of Kolkata. Maharishi Debendranath, the father of Nobel laureate Rabindranath Tagore, was a significant supporter of the Brahmo Samaj revolution.

Such studies instilled a sense of practicality in the children, especially Abhi. He was a pragmatic child who often used this trait to conceal his deep emotional side. When he successfully secured admission to a prestigious institute through an India-wide engineering entrance test, Abhi found himself torn between electrical and civil engineering during his first year. Ultimately, he chose civil engineering because he appreciated symmetry and tangible creativity. These fields seemed practical and lucrative; however, Abhi was as stubborn as his father. It was likely why the two were both the best of friends and the best of foes.

Abhi had frequent issues with his college professors and later with his first boss. Sumati had long known that Abhi would be an honest but somewhat difficult employee. He was proactive and always sought ways to improve the status quo, often unintentionally rubbing his seniors the wrong way. Despite his contentious attitude, Abhi's popularity among women remained unaffected. After completing business school in Los Angeles, he decided to accept an offer from a local entrepreneur, George Nelson.

Chapter 6

December 26, 2019, Glencoe, a suburb of Chicago

It was the morning after Christmas. Bhavna had woken up late after a long week of dealing with issues in her research project. The previous night she called home to let her dad know she would be late, but his voice sounded different—something was not right. When her dad shared the news, Bhavna broke down. For the next four hours, she cried—cried because she had lost her best friend. There were so many memories they had created together, so many things left undone, and so many plans for the future. Who would she talk to now? Who would she joke around with?

Her dad had contacted his legal friend, Stein, who specialized in cleaning crime scenes. Stein's firm was called "Tony's," a name that sounded more like a bar than a forensic service. While he mostly worked privately, he occasionally took assignments from the city law enforcement.

Stein: Ajit, we can start the forensics on the site.

Ajit didn't respond. The news had shaken the entire Sengupta family—Borda (Shekhar), who seemed to have everything going right with a promising entrepreneurial future, had taken his own life. A suicide note had been sent to the police department. The family struggled to understand the motive, wondering if there were repressed emotions that no one had noticed. Borda often hung out with some of his old school friends and invested money in speculation, occasionally dealing with people of questionable repute.

All night, Bhavna kept receiving messages from her parents, each suggesting different reasons why Shekhar might have taken his own life. There was even speculation that it could have been a murder disguised as a suicide.

This morning, as she continued her internet search on Borda's whereabouts, an email hit her inbox - "Hi Bhavna"—caught her attention. The sender was "Abhi in LA." It seemed suspicious, almost like spam or a phishing attempt.

The email read:

"Hi Bhavna,

I am Abhi. I got your email ID from my parents. They wanted to connect us so that we can assess the suitability towards entering into a holy matrimony.

If interested, please email me."

It felt impersonal and generic—like something that could be sent to a hundred other people. There was no effort to personalize it, no indication that he knew anything about her, yet it was direct and to the point.

Her first instinct was to delete it immediately, but she hesitated. Deleting it wouldn't stop Abhi from sending such curt, thoughtless emails to others. Frustrated, she decided to write back.

"Assessment of suitability can only be done if we meet in person. I don't see any reason why I would do so. It would be insensible to try to gather information about you when all I see are a bunch of red flags. I'm certain these red flags would become stop signs if we met. You'll find better women. I'm sorry, but we are not meant for each other. Good luck. "

Bhavna was like a skeptical ant in a sugar bowl, resisting any help to escape. She often struggled with finding that special someone she could envision spending her life with.

That evening, she looked forward to catching up with Karan. It was a cold evening, though there was no snow. Karan had tentatively accepted her invite. Bhavna debated whether to call Karan or wait for his call. Thirty minutes passed, and there was still no response from him.

Finally, she decided to call and left a long message. Just two minutes after hanging up, her phone rang. She was ready to deliver her prepared speech to Karan, but it wasn't him this time.

"This is Bhavna."

"Hi, Bhavna, I'm Abhi."

"Abhi—who?"

"Bhavna, I wrote an email earlier. My parents gave me your phone number and email address."

"Yes, I got that. But I'm in the middle of something."

"To give you a quick rundown, I got my civil engineering degree from India, went into consulting, and then business school in Los Angeles."

"Great, but can we talk over the weekend?"

"I sell professional services to public agencies—services they don't need."

"And how do you do that?" Bhavna wasn't in the mood to understand intricacies, but it was a calming diversion from the deep cloud of sadness cast over the family.

"Sometimes by looking into their needs. Other times, by identifying unspent money in their budget."

While she was talking to Abhi, another call came in. Karan's number showed up on the screen.

"I have to take this other call. Can I call you back, or can you hold?"

"Why don't you call me back?" Abhi knew from experience that it was time to end the conversation.

"Sure... I'll call you."

She picked up Karan's call.

"I'm sorry, Bhavna, for being late. I heard about your brother—I'm very sorry to hear that. I'll miss him."

"Very shocking," Bhavna acknowledged. She burst into tears, but then wiped them away and stayed quiet.

"Last week, my car was giving me problems—but today, it just wouldn't start. So now I'm here on Green Bay Road, outside this coffee shop. It's late, but do you want to talk about it?"

She explained how the cops had discovered her brother's body with a finger cut off. They were still investigating how it all happened.

Bhavna also got a chance to talk to Karan after a year. A year ago, Karan had taken a chance and tried to kiss her, but she had refused. To avoid any awkwardness, they focused on their own worlds and avoided discussing Karan's advances. They still bumped into each other occasionally and exchanged words, but never more than that. Not long after, Karan started dating Priya, whom he met in a social setting.

Karan was amicable in most social situations and often agreed with what others said. Sumati considered him the most balanced among the three—not because he was the oldest, but because he reacted calmly even to the most heart-wrenching events and handled curveballs with a level head. While he was often perceived as introverted, he knew what to say and when to say it, without ever fully letting his guard down.

At the same time, he was honing his psychic abilities by consulting with others who had similar experiences. He wanted to see if he could connect with someone else's dreams or even those from the past. Perhaps that way, he could find out what had truly happened to Borda.

* * *

Abhi was getting better at embedding romantic escapes in an otherwise stressful post-Christmas day with Lewis.

Abhi stared at the bright-colored handwriting on his to-do list, debating whether to call and send her wishes or simply ignore her. Maybe ignoring her would spark a bit of an argument. Abhi was really hoping they were the real thing—a little chaos couldn't hurt, right? He shrugged. After a long pause, he dialed her number but quickly hung up when he noticed Lewis staring down at him.

"In my office... now."

Abhi's face flushed red as he entered the office, unsure of what to expect. Lewis was seated on his desk, his expression stoic.

"Have a seat."

"I'm good—"

"Have a seat, Abhi."

Abhi sank into the chair, his hands interlocked tightly to hide their trembling.

"What were you doing on the phone?"

Abhi's mind raced before recalling his attempt to set up a virtual meeting for some of their bigger clients. That part of his to-do list surfaced just in time.

"The clients... I was trying to call the clients..."

Lewis blinked slowly, his gaze fixed on Abhi. "Any word from Borda, huh?"

Abhi nodded instinctively, then quickly shook his head.

"No, nothing."

"Okay." Lewis walked to his chair and produced a box. "This came in for you. A taxi driver said you dropped it."

"Taxi driver?" Abhi raised a brow.

Lewis shrugged lazily. "You apparently tipped him too well—he felt he had to bring it back."

Abhi's forehead creased. He couldn't remember taking a taxi, let alone leaving behind a package.

Lewis slid the box toward him. It was a cube wrapped in plain brown paper with no identifying note—just a simple, nondescript package.

"Want to open it?" Lewis asked.

Abhi stared at the package, his heart pounding like an engine about to stall.

"No."

* * *

Ross was back in Chicago as well for Christmas with his folks.

After his call with his old pal, Ross took a moment to reflect. His friend Karan had been fed the biggest lie by some of the investigators. With his sharp understanding of persuasion and human behavior, Ross could sense deception from a mile away. He knew Karan's absence had deeper reasons than it appeared.

Ross made a quick call to the Chicago taxi company. He had a simple request. Shortly after, two emails arrived. One was from the taxi firm, detailing the taxicab Anurag Roy had used. It included the taxi's plate number, the driver—Luke Owens—and the other passengers Luke had picked up before Anurag. Ross skimmed over everything, focusing solely on the driver's information.

As he dialed Luke's number, he opened the second email.

He rushed out of his office, eyes glued to the letter.

Boom!

In an instant, the entire building housing Ross's office erupted in flames. Within minutes, it burned to the ground.

* * *

Abhi bolted the door the moment he stepped into his apartment. He had been sweating all the way from work, glancing over his shoulder a thousand times, certain he was being followed. The box remained tucked under his arm as he walked past the mall, the bridge, and several coffee shops. He kept moving until he reached the crimson-red door of his minimalist apartment.

Rushing into the bathroom, he splashed his face with water from the sink.

"It's just a dream," he muttered, desperately trying to convince himself. The call from Borda, the ride to Welling Trade, the gunshots, the fall—everything felt like a twisted, self-induced fantasy. Yet doubt began to creep in. Was there a power he had but never knew?

Growing up, Abhi had envied his siblings for their abilities. Chandra could travel through pictures, and Karan could navigate dreams. Meanwhile, Abhi felt powerless, convinced he had no special talent. Even when his parents assured him he had abilities, he didn't believe them.

Now, staring at the package resting in the water closet, Abhi wasn't sure what to believe anymore.

He fumbled through his phone. Someone had tampered with it—everything was gone, vanished, just like when he had tried to show it to his boss. Abhi was still confused about the whole thing. He remembered checking the address the night before. Who would have wiped his phone? How had he survived that fall? How did he end up in the US? And what on earth was in that package?

Abhi dropped the package on his dining table, which doubled as his reading table. Taking a deep breath, he tore it open.

* * *

Meanwhile, on the same day, in another part of Chicago, Chandra waited for her boyfriend after they had returned from New Delhi the night before. They planned to celebrate New Year's in

Downtown Chicago with the two brothers before heading back to Fullerton. It was their twentieth month together, and she wore a green sweater that had belonged to her dad.

Chandra glanced at his photo on her phone. She had his eyes. Wearing the cashmere sweater made her feel closer to him, as if they shared a spiritual bond. Her father had been fascinated by spiritual realities, drawn to Tantric philosophies and Mayan culture. According to her mother, he had traveled to Guatemala, read dense texts on their beliefs, and conducted out-of-body experiments with his friends from childhood.

Chandra felt a sense of pride—she was following in her dad's footsteps. Although she had graduated in computer science from a leading university in the US, she was eager to pursue a doctorate in parapsychology, metaphysics, or a field that pushed the boundaries of her mind. Something that bridged psychology and computing. So far, everything was going according to plan.

All she wanted now was to spend a long, romantic night.

Her phone rang.

"Hello?"

"You kept me waiting..." Chandra said. It was Pierre.

"I'm so sorry. I vos held op. Will be there in 15 minutes... stadium... Starbucks on 55th?"

"I'm walking toward that—how was the meeting?"

"I have a surprise."

* * *

After playing phone tag, Karan finally got a text from Abhi. He couldn't help but wonder what had happened to his brother. When they finally met, Abhi was out of breath.

"Let's get out of here," Abhi said urgently.

Karan opened the door, and they drove off. The roads were dark, and Karan had a growing sense that someone was following them. Abhi's hands were smeared with blood, and he kept rambling about a package.

Ring... ring.

Karan jolted awake—it had been a dream. Priya was calling. If only she would stop being so mushy and start acting like a normal woman. She did everything too much—smiled too much, talked too much.

Just as he was about to answer, a text from Abhi popped up, asking to meet at a bar. It was a relief. Karan quickly told Priya he'd be spending time with his brother. Any excuse to get a break from his fiancée was welcome. Besides, there was something he wanted to discuss with Abhi.

Karan had picked the bar. He was greeted by a sea of people, their bodies swaying to a song he found borderline inappropriate. The bar itself was unremarkable, but the air carried a strange mix of beer and candy—like the owner had once intended to sell fruit juice but switched to beer for a more reliable cash flow.

A few minutes in, Karan wondered if he could bear the place. Still, heading back to a dull home and a fiancée who seemed to thrive on monotony didn't seem appealing either. Maybe this place wasn't so bad after all.

He maneuvered through the crowd, weaving between bodies until he reached the table where Abhi said he'd be.

Karan frowned. It was empty.

He's still not here... always late...

Karan was pushing through the crowd toward table forty-five when someone tugged at his shirt. He turned sharply, his hand ready to swat away the intruder.

His irritation faded as he saw Abhi's flustered face.

"We have to get the hell out of here," Abhi said breathlessly.

Chapter 7

December 26, 2019, Chicago

Right after Abhi left his flat, he dashed into a cab, watching two police cars halt at his front porch.

"Go, go, go..."

"Where to?" the driver asked.

"Just keep driving."

As the taxi sped down the road, Abhi caught his breath in the backseat. He realized he didn't have his credit cards—he'd left them near the TV while ordering food earlier. Desperate, he voice-dialed his mom, his last resort.

"Abhi?"

"Mom... I need your help..."

"What's wrong, son?"

"I may need your ATM card. I'll pay back by—"

The line went dead. Sumati was on a Chicago bound flight and she had drained her cell phone battery.

Abhi gritted his teeth. His mother had disconnected the call. He saw the driver staring at him through the rearview mirror. Abhi shot him a glare.

"What are you looking at? I'll pay my cab fare. Merry Christmas, and thank you."

The driver focused on the road. Abhi thought he knew what the man was thinking—some broke Indian student trying to pull a stunt. But Abhi barely had the time to pull any stunt now, not after what he had seen in the package. It had left him shell-shocked. With the cops at his front door, he knew he was in big trouble. What he had left on his table would haunt him forever. The image was now carved into his memory. He racked his brain, wondering what to do and who could help.

The moment Abhi had ripped open the package, he found a red box. On it was a handwritten note in uppercase letters. Abhi's eyes darkened as he read it:

DO YOU WANT TO END UP LIKE HIM?

P.S. WE'RE WATCHING YOU.

DON'T GO TO THE COPS AS THEY WILL ARREST YOU... AND THEN WE WILL KILL YOU.

Abhi's hands trembled as he dropped the note and opened the box. A foul smell hit him instantly, making his spine crawl with thick shivers. Wrapped in blood-soaked fabric lay a severed middle finger, a faint, discolored ring mark still visible. There was another note, scrawled in what looked like blood:

BORDA SHOWED US THIS. WE SENT HIM AWAY FOR GOOD.

* * *

"Are we being followed?"

Karan asked himself as his car sped down a different route. Beside him, Abhi sat in silence, his face damp with sweat. They had bailed out of the bar and were now heading to a more secure location Karan had in mind. Abhi hadn't spoken since they got into the car.

After several tense minutes on the road, they pulled up outside an electric gate. A security guard stepped out, saluted Karan, and signaled to a man inside the penthouse. They were granted entry.

Karan drove through, his eyes tracing the massive structure that stood before them — a cherry-red wood cabin blending with the pitch-black forest behind. Servers moved behind a bar inside, and a few guests lingered, drinks in hand. This was what a strong network could afford, Karan mused, tempted to say it aloud but held back. He glanced at Abhi, whose gaze was still locked on the glove box. *For heaven's sake, be impressed!*

Finally seated at their reserved spot, Karan studied his brother, waiting for him to speak. Abhi remained silent, looking worn out — like a man on the run for his life.

"I also wanted to see you," Karan said, taking a sip from his glass, his eyes lingering on a waitress in a fitted dress. Abhi massaged his temple, staring at his untouched drink, the ice already melting away.

"But you are yet to tell me why you wanted us to meet...and what was it you said about being followed?"

Abhi looked around, his face buried behind his palm.

"I...I need..." Abhi sighed. "...to catch my breath."

"Of course," Karan nodded. "In that case, it may surprise you to know that we'll be securing a multi-million-dollar deal, for some human analytics research, from Legacy Inc. Finally, we can get our EB5 Green cards."

Karan beamed proudly, waiting to see the excitement in his brother's eyes. Abhi said nothing. He simply stared before slowly lifting his head.

"Abhi...what's wrong?"

Abhi's eyes were moist, tears racing down his cheeks — his eyes glistened like crystals.

"Is everything ok? Did something go wrong at work?"

Abhi shook his head, reclining into the chair.

"No." Abhi inhaled and downed the glass of old-fashioned whisky. It burned the back of his throat.

Karan's eyes shook as he nodded. "If you say so…tell me, how's…how's life?"

"Fine." Abhi said, refilling his glass, his eyes still moist. "How's Priya?"

"She's... she's ok. Talked to her lately?"

"Not since New Delhi, no."

"Hmmh." Karan nodded, fingering the rim of his glass. Both men sat in silence for a minute.

"There's…there's a problem."

Karan looked at his brother, hearing him stutter.

"A problem? Let me go first. I spoke to my friend, Ross. Ross is a private investigator. He thinks…he thinks we may be able to reopen the case."

"The case…"

"Yes, Dad's case."

Abhi stared at his brother's drink, his own reflection distorted on the glass. This wasn't the conversation he wanted to have. As a matter of fact, he was far from this conversation…far away… somewhere else. He didn't like talking about Dad. Not that he hated him or anything. He just didn't like it.

"He's agreed to meet us," Karan continued. "I've made arrangements for us to meet—"

"Somebody's trying to kill me."

The air between them grew heavy, the clinking of cutlery and muffled chatter filling the background. Karan's breathing quickened, a screw in his head threatening to come loose.

"Someone wants to kill me," Abhi repeated, his face stoic even as his cheeks began to grow wet.

Karan shifted in his seat. "Kill you?"

"Someone called Borda dies, and I get a middle finger in a box sent to me by a special courier," Abhi informed his brother. "I fear that our lives… for sure, my life may be in d—"

Abhi's phone rang.

Karan glanced at it — ringing for nearly twenty times.

"You're not going to answer it?"

Abhi blinked, silent.

"Don't!" Abhi said, but Karan had already picked up.

"Hello?"

"A—Abhi... eetz me…"

"Who is this?"

"Eetz Pierre… Shandra…"

"We'll see you in a bit, Pierre. Now's a bad time — Abhi seems to be running from someone who's after his life. I'll let you know more when we meet in the next couple of hours."

"Wait, Shandra... eetz Shandra… someone tried to kidnap her."

Karan pressed the phone tighter to his ear, his eyes widening. The line went dead.

"We've got to go…"

Abhi looked up at his brother, his wet eyes questioning. "Why…"

"Chandra might be in trouble. Seems today isn't our family's day."

As they drove, they kept trying to reach Pierre and Chandra, hoping they were still on Magnificent Mile. They also tried to contact their mother.

Chapter 8

December 27, 2019, Chicago – 2: 00 AM

Pierre is dead.

Abhi clutched his face, staring blankly at the doctor, while his brother tried to reach their mother over the phone. The doctor had spoken those words with a straight, composed face.

"I'm sorry, Abhi, he never made it."

Abhi struggled to find words. For a moment, it felt like a heavy weight clamped on his throat. No matter how hard he tried, no words came out. After a few moments of suppressed sorrow, he finally spoke.

"And Chandra? What about her?"

"She took a lot of damage — her ribs, her skull... There's a chance her spinal cord may be affected too. She's still in a coma. It could take days, even months, before we get her back..."

That was as far as Abhi could hear. His mind drifted away, wanting nothing more than to rush into the intensive care unit and see his sister. Heaven knew how long she would be in there.

"Thank you, doctor," he heard Karan say. "We'll wait."

"Please, let me know if you need anything," the doctor said as he turned to leave.

* * *

December 24, 2019, Cairo, Illinois

A skinny man stepped out to take out the trash. He noticed a truck parked not far from his house — an unusual sight in the quiet neighborhood that rarely attracted attention. It was the reason he had bought the property years ago. His gaze lingered on the man inside the truck, who had a camera strap around his neck. Maybe a reporter, he thought. When their eyes met, he quickly tossed the trash and made his way back to the house. By the time he reached the door, the reporter was already in his yard.

"Hi there," the reporter greeted.

The man responded with a gruff sound, the kind animals make when challenged but uninterested.

"Can't help but admire the lawn. It's lush green," the reporter remarked.

"Are you selling fertilizer or just nosy?" the skinny man replied with a smirk.

"I'm analyzing this field, thought I could get your take. Maybe over a few beers?"

"Nah, I'm good. Thanks, though."

"Alright then. I guess I'll see you around."

"Are you writing a story or what?" the man asked, his curiosity faint yet guarded.

"Sorry?" the reporter responded.

"I said, are you writing a story? You said you're a reporter."

"It depends — you don't seem like the type who'd want me writing your story."

The lanky man scratched his neck. "Why's that?"

"I don't know. Maybe we could discuss it over a few beers."

"Haha, alright. I know a great bar nearby."

"I'm sure you do," the reporter replied, as the man excused himself and disappeared inside for what felt like ages. When he finally emerged an hour later, he wore cleaner clothes, and his week-old stubble was gone.

"Figured I'd clean up, just in case you take pictures for your story."

"Oh, sure, sure," the reporter chuckled.

They strolled out to the truck and drove to a local bar known for its happy hour. Once they settled in and ordered a pitcher of draft beer, the reporter extended his hand.

"I'm Ross, by the way."

"Owen."

"Owens?"

"Owen," the lanky man corrected. "So, what story are you writing?"

"I'm not supposed to talk about it," Ross whispered, glancing around cautiously. "But I have a feeling you can keep a secret, can't you, Owen?"

"Usually, I'd say no, but sure. I can keep secrets."

"I'll tell you mine, but then you'll have to tell me yours," Ross said, refilling Owen's glass.

"I'm an open book. Go ahead."

"Alright," Ross began. "I'm writing a story about abandoned homes and neighborhoods. It's for a magazine. Supposedly, they're curious about the big secrets—trying to find some scientific explanation for why places just get left behind. Nobody cares about politics or conspiracy nuts anymore. They sent me to this city to pick up leads, but I see nothing."

"Hmm." Owen muttered, raising his glass. "Here's to a wasted publication effort."

Their glasses clinked.

"I hope it's not my time, huh?" Ross chuckled.

"You said it," Owen replied.

"I knew a man once. He was broke—dead broke. Had a wife who loved him. You know what he'd do? Beat her up. And their kid just watched—watched his old man beat his mama up. One day, the old man gets home and tells his wife and kid to dig. They dig this big hole in their front yard, and he buries something. Won't tell a soul what it is. Then, one day, he goes out and never comes back. At least, not alive. Dies without a dime to his name. His wife soon follows, leaving their broke kid to fend for himself. Nobody knew the old man had buried millions in that yard. It's still there, and no one knows."

"Hmm, very interesting," Ross said, sipping his beer.

"Would that make a nice story?"

"Of course. How'd you hear that?"

"Why, does it matter?"

Ross nodded. "For these publishers, yeah. They need data, evidence—proof it's real. Otherwise, it's just a fable."

Owen took a sip, shaking his head. "I don't trust you. But who gives a damn about trust?"

Both men burst into laughter.

"Well," Ross chuckled, "when I'm dead, you better bury me right."

"Haha, you're trusting me to bury you right?"

"Yeah, like those millions that old man buried—so nobody knows. Just two drunk fools, huh?"

Owen grinned, wiping his mouth. "I like you. You're a good person," he said, standing up. "I wanna show you something. Come on."

Ross, half-drunk but curious, paid for the drinks, and the two headed to his truck. Owen climbed in through the window, and Ross watched, amused.

"Hey, what are we doing, my friend?" Ross slurred.

"Come on, we're going to write the best story of your life."

Minutes later, they arrived at Owen's house. Owen hopped out and paused. "Do you have a camera?"

"Never a day without one," Ross replied, holding up his phone.

"Good... good." Owen said, his eyes sharp with intention.

Ross followed as Owen led him to the backyard. Owen disappeared inside briefly, then returned with a shovel.

Ross raised an eyebrow. "What're you doing, Owen?"

"Just watch... and make sure you get this on camera."

"You want me to film you digging?"

"Photos, video—whatever you like."

"Hey, man, seriously, what are you up to?"

"Trust me on this, beer buddy," Owen said, driving the spade into the soil.

"On camera!" he called out.

Ross pulled out his phone, switching between photos and recording. His mind wandered—this was easily the strangest interview he'd ever conducted. Owen seemed like a guy who didn't get much company, an oddball willing to dig up dirt at midnight just to impress a stranger. Yet, Ross couldn't help but feel a rush of excitement. Maybe there was a story here.

Owen finally stopped, his face streaked with dirt and sweat.

"You didn't have to do this, Owen," Ross said, lowering his phone.

"Come take a look, Ross."

Owen pulled a sack from the earth, dusted it off, and opened it. Ross's jaw dropped.

"No freaking way."

Owen's face lit up with a proud smile.

"These are diamonds, Owen. Freaking diamonds."

"Yeah. They're worth millions," Owen replied calmly.

"Jeez, man, is it even safe to have this out in the open?" Ross said, glancing nervously around.

"Come off it, there's nothing to worry about. This hood is a ghost town," Owen said, tucking the sack back into the soil.

"You didn't really have to show me those," Ross said as they walked back to the front yard.

"Did you take photos of it?"

"Hell no! That's like the number one way to get killed."

"For real?"

"For real, man. But that story about the old man—was it for real?"

"No, I... I made it up. Haha."

"Smart one. Hey, Owen, I couldn't help but notice an abandoned taxi on the road there. Is it yours?"

"No, it was my dad's. Passed away a long time ago."

"Whoa. Sorry about that. Death—death is such a freak."

"Nah, I'm glad he's dead. Was the best thing that ever happened to me."

Ross nodded.

"Ross."

"Yeah?"

"You can keep a secret, right? Those diamonds in the yard—they're not what they seem..."

"What do you mean?"

"You're not planning to make a story out of this, are you? 'Cause, seriously, it could get me killed."

"Of course not," Ross said, slipping his pad into his pocket. "Why would anyone want you dead?"

"You have no idea what I've done, pal. No idea. But I'll tell you..."

"Tell me what?"

"About the diamonds—how I got them."

Ross listened closely as Owen revealed everything.

Minutes later, they walked quietly to Ross's truck. It felt like something had been lost—like something had gone terribly wrong. Yet, one of them was only pretending. And it wasn't Owen.

"You're not gonna tell anyone, right?" Owen asked.

"God, no. I swear—I won't say a word," Ross replied as he started the engine.

"Guess you'll come around again, huh? Maybe this time I'll treat you to a beer."

"Haha, sure," Ross said. "See you around."

"Yeah, see you around." With that, Owen turned to leave.

Ross pulled out his camera and snapped a quick shot of the house. Then, he discreetly switched off the audio recorder hidden in his shirt. He sighed, satisfied with a job well done.

"Hey."

Ross jolted as Owen reappeared.

"Yeah, I startled you. Sorry. Just wondering... you said you're a reporter, right?"

"Yeah, sure..."

Owen rubbed his mouth, his eyes fixed on Ross's camera.

"Can I see some ID?"

* * *

December 27, 2019, Chicago

Abhi's head spun with a thousand thoughts at the hospital. He sat up, suddenly thinking back to when he worked for his old boss, George.

He had heard countless times from George how George made it. The subprime real estate market in the US took a major hit, and the housing bubble was about to crash in 2007. The banks had taken risks by buying asset-backed securities and collateralized debt obligations, hoping for better returns, but they were wrong. The entrepreneurial spirit had taken a back seat. Restaurants in the suburbs of Los Angeles had a resonating emptiness, shelves full of inventory, and eager attendants with no customers. There was an undercurrent of sadness, concern, and uncertainty behind their smiles.

Still, the bad real estate market brought a ray of hope for people like George, who didn't want to let the recession go to waste.

George had outsourced services, realizing the competitive advantage of setting up an operation in India. He had some of the best templates in place and experience writing policies and procedures for public agencies in the architecture, engineering, and construction fields. George started an AutoCAD shop in 2008 from his bedroom, and it took off even before he could properly set it up. In less than two years, he had over fifty utility clients in California, all seeking lower costs from George's offshore model. His business grew rapidly—at one point, he had 200 employees.

But soon, copycats emerged, taking business away from George. So much so that he had to let go of many employees.

It was at a time like this that Abhi walked into his life. Abhi was looking for a job that could sponsor his H1B visa and promised to grow the business quickly. After just a two-minute conversation, George asked him to start. Abhi wasn't all talk—everything he said, he did.

George was exceedingly kind at the beginning, but gradually, he changed, becoming the exact opposite of what he once stood for. He never acknowledged how Abhi had expanded the customer base. After three years of working with George, Abhi had learned a lot about business operations and managing entrepreneurs. He had considered going solo, but his work visa status wouldn't allow it.

George had a classic type A entrepreneurial personality, something he took pride in. Employees, however, speculated that it might actually be an undiagnosed attention deficit disorder. Almost every morning began with rants like:

"Abhi, did you get the P.O. from Pasadena?"

Abhi would either stay silent or nod.

"I think that is still sitting in Accounts Payable, and when I..." Abhi would start, but George would interrupt.

"When are you meeting with the City of Manhattan Beach?"

"I have scheduled it for next month..."

"Why isn't it in the sales report?"

I have already entered it."

"Are you over 80% of your quota for this month?"

"I'm trying. Still have some proposals going out tomorrow."

"You know that if you don't make 200 G, no paycheck for you this month."

In situations like these, Abhi often chose to stay quiet. His visa status had stripped him of much of his confidence and quick retorts, and George knew exactly which buttons to push.

George's wife, Mary, was one of the few reasons Abhi tolerated George. He often wondered what had drawn her to George in the first place. Her smile felt like a rare downpour in the sun-scorched deserts of the Inland Empire—brief but revitalizing. Her latest passion was ballroom dancing, but George never took her out or joined her classes. Instead, he had her attend dance classes with friends and even employees. Once, George had suggested that Abhi accompany Mary to a Foxtrot class. Abhi declined, citing other commitments.

Things took a dark turn one night during a party at George's house. Abhi was there to discuss contract details with a new client. He had just finished the conversation and was about to leave when Mary walked in. George suddenly slapped her, yanked her hair, and spat out a vile insult.

Smack!

The sound reverberated through the room. Abhi's stomach churned, his blood rushing.

Leave now, Abhi... Leave...

He couldn't believe what he had witnessed — George hitting his wife so openly, so brutally. Yet, Abhi didn't move. His rage swelled as he watched the scene unfold.

"Don't do this, George," Abhi said, his voice steady.

George turned to face him, eyes bloodshot and wild, as if possessed.

"Get lost." George said dismissively, his hand still clamped hard at Mary's throat. Abhi walked slowly, his chest pounding, hoping to somehow go back and settle this without incurring George's anger.

"Please, George, I beg you… stop." Abhi said, his eyes starting to water as his cheeks trembled.

George was still strangling his wife. "Don't be a wimp. Crawl back to whatever hole you fell from… off you go—"

Abhi intercepted a wild swing before it could land on Mary. George never had the chance to finish his sentence; he slipped and fell on his face. Abhi didn't fully grasp what had happened until George stopped moving.

The rest of that night had been a blur. George had died from the head injury after his fall, and Mary would spend the next few years a widow. And Abhi? He knew he was done with that kind of compassion — things like that complicated your life. He may have had a thing for Mary, but he wasn't sure he could risk being vulnerable.

Abhi looked up and returned to the present. Karan was seated next to him now. They remained there, silent.

* * *

Hours passed, and Karan tried convincing himself that everything would be fine. He had informed Priya about what happened and had tried reaching their mom, who was on a flight to the US to spend the first few months of the New Year with her kids. He wondered how she'd react to the news that Chandra and Pierre had been hit by a driver who fled the scene.

Karan chose not to mention the strange dream he had the night before — a dream where he'd seen a truck hit a couple. He glanced at his brother. Abhi kept his eyes fixed on the door where the doctor had disappeared. He looked ready to wait for hours, even days, if needed.

Finally, the door to the operating room opened, and the doctor hurried out.

"I'm afraid we may have a problem. Please come with me."

The brothers followed him into the ICU, where the nurses and medical assistants stepped aside to make room. Karan stepped forward. Chandra lay motionless on the bed, tubes connected to her body.

"Hey, Chandra." Karan's voice cracked, but he was grateful she was still alive.

The doctor reappeared from behind.

"I thought it would be best for you to see her condition firsthand. When your sister wakes up from the coma, she may... I regret to say... experience some physical difficulties with movement."

"What kind of difficulties?" Abhi asked.

"During surgery, we discovered severe damage to her spine. The discs are badly displaced. I'm afraid it may take years for your sister to walk again."

* * *

Bhavna's parents had often brought up the topic of marriage, reminding her that her biological clock was ticking faster than ever. The pressure grew heavier as two of her close friends, Shivani and Madhavi, had already married and settled down nearly two years ago. When Bhavna ran into Crystal at an alumni meetup, she found herself initiated into the world of online dating. Crystal's horror stories about hookups from bars, clubs, and malls convinced Bhavna to give it a try. She also joined an Indian matrimony site at her mother's insistence. Ever since, Bhavna and Crystal had been comparing notes.

Even though the whole Sengupta house was dark and quiet that occasional *you've got mail* alert got her away from the grim situation and motivated her to respond. It wasn't clear if with her it was a case of delayed grief, where sadness would manifest later, rather than immediately after the loss. Or perhaps she was not yet fully processing her loss. But that pushed her to connect with Crystal and get some comic relief. Bhavna shared her online conversations with Abhi, even reading one email aloud:

"As regards relationships, I think I am looking for small pleasures that can be attained in a variety of low-key and unambitious ways. At the same time, I am looking to put in a lot of passion, persistence, and perseverance (Abhi's 3 Ps) in what we do—whether it be managing day-to-day activities, creating something synergistically, or even doing dishes. Being ambitious is good, but we have to plan our plan Bs as there should be contingency routes always—and that's again where an understanding and mature partner can help. Everyone is impulsive and rash in some decisions while very calculating in others—a good partnership can help even out those decisions. Exploring new things together—places, history, arts, cuisines, films—is also something I seek in a partnership. And, of course, sharing values and compassion for the world is a big item on my checklist."

Crystal listened intently before smirking, "He seems serious. I'd go out with him if you don't." Her laughter was followed by silence. Realizing the gravity of Bhavna's hesitation, she softened her tone, "I know you have a lot going on, but maybe let him know what's on your mind—it'll save both of you from any blind spots."

Since she began communicating with Abhi, Bhavna found herself intrigued by his thoughts, beliefs, and clear goals. Yet, a part of her resented the idea of an arranged marriage, especially with someone whose upbringing differed so much from hers. When she voiced her hesitation, Abhi had responded, "*Parents are only interfaces here. The onus to decide is still on us—it's just that the tire-kicking process is shorter—actually much shorter here.*"

His perspective lingered in her mind, leaving her both curious and conflicted.

* * *

December 27, 2019, Chicago

That morning, Abhi arrived at the office a little later than usual, still reeling from the news about Chandra's health. He had spent the night at the hospital—too shaken to go home—and the staff had kindly offered him a bed. Abhi had insisted Karan leave, promising to stay by Chandra's side. Yet, when he woke up later than expected, he saw Karan still there, sitting silently beside their sister. With a quick change of clothes, Abhi headed to work, arriving past eleven, cautiously looking out for Lewis. Fortunately, his boss wasn't around.

Abhi buried himself in his tasks, trying to distract himself from the chaos of the last few days. Bhavna had left a few messages, but he barely had the energy to respond. Hours drifted by until it was time to leave, but Abhi stayed back, his mind piecing together the events. Could it be that Borda's killers had orchestrated the attack on Chandra and Pierre? The thought made his heart clench, tight and painful.

The report had said Chandra and Pierre were on their way to the stadium when a pickup truck struck them. It hit Pierre hard before speeding away. Chandra had passed out on the spot. Pierre, barely conscious, had managed to call Abhi—just before he died.

As Abhi wrapped up for the day, Lewis walked in, offering a brief nod as he passed. Abhi nodded back, relieved there were no sarcastic questions or impossible demands that would leave him fumbling for answers.

His phone buzzed—Bhavna was calling. Abhi hesitated, debating whether to tell her he was busy and—

"How's it going?"

Abhi nearly stumbled when he saw Lewis peeking into his cubicle.

"Lewis... you s—"

"Scared you?"

"Startled—you startled me."

"Right, sorry... Any word from Mulligan and Borda?"

Abhi's throat tightened, memories of Borda's finger tearing through his skull flashing back.

"Uh, no. Not a word."

"Right, right... Seen the news lately?"

"What news?"

"It's nothing. Never mind." Lewis turned away, leaving Abhi with a lingering unease.

"Yeah, see you around, boss." Abhi said, his phone starting to vibrate.

"Oh, and Abhi..." Lewis called back.

"Yes?"

Lewis cleared his throat, his relaxed face assuming a stoic stance as he said coolly:

"You're fired."

* * *

Abhi's legs wobbled as he stepped out of the office, his mind a blank slate of panic. Who would sponsor his visa now? Did Homeland Security think he killed Borda? How would he see Chandra if he had to go back? Where would he find another job? Everything felt up in the air. He clutched the carton with his belongings tightly as he left the office he once saw himself leading. His career had hit rock bottom.

His phone rang for the tenth time.

Bhavna.

Abhi had dodged her calls all day, but now, at this bleak hour, she was calling again. Against his better judgment, he picked up.

"Abhi! I've been calling all day. I'm in the city! I was hoping we could meet up—"

That was all Abhi heard before he cut in. His response was brief, final. When the call ended, he knew Bhavna would never reach out again.

It started to rain.

Chapter 9

December 26, 2019, Chicago – Noon

Chandra had followed her dream of attending a leading American university for her master's. When she saw her final scores online, she couldn't believe she had made it to the Dean's list. It seemed like everything was going as planned. She had informed the family of their safe arrival in Chicago—they were staying at a hotel near Abhi's flat. Although Abhi had insisted they stay with him, Pierre preferred the independence of a hotel. After unloading his luggage, Pierre had left for his meeting, while Chandra took a quick nap.

All she could think about was telling Pierre the news. Pierre had a meeting at the University of Chicago.

She raced through the university campus, crossing streets with her heart pounding, to reach the Starbucks on 55th Street—close to Stagg Field, or the stadium as some called it. This wasn't the Starbucks where they had first met. Their first encounter was at the orientation day in the induction hall, just a two-minute walk from there. It had been love at first sight.

Jean Pierre left the professor's office with a rolled-up paper in his fist and walked toward the bike rack. He rode as fast as he could to reach Starbucks, but Vincent, a fellow French PhD candidate, stopped him on the way.

Vincent tapped Jean Pierre's back and said, "Jean Pierre, cava?"

"Bien et vous?" replied Jean Pierre. He didn't even bother to lift his head. His inexpressive face conveyed the message, "I'm good, and you?" but truly meant, "I have to go."

Students and job seekers were eager to apply for work permits, especially given the current situation where these visas—necessary to work in the US—were becoming a rare commodity. Jean Pierre, who had been waiting for his dream work permit after receiving a job offer from a leading electrical utility firm in the US, finally got it. There was a fear that the employer might rescind the offer if the wait continued, but there it was—the multicolored visa pasted on his passport. It was Pierre's day.

Jean Pierre rode his bike frantically to reach his destination, but he was stopped by Professor Wilkinson, who wanted to congratulate him on his work. In Professor Wilkinson, Jean saw a great friend and advisor—it was through the professor's connections that Jean Pierre had received the job offer. Professor Wilkinson knew Chandra as well and had been planning a trip to India with both Pierre and her.

Pierre worked with Professor Wilkinson on designing an algorithm that analyzed accounts, identified irregular transactions, and traced them back to fraudulent money laundering activities. To build the model, they had obtained data from a few banks. However, when they tested the model on data from banks in Tunisia, they found numerous irregularities, which Pierre had shared with the Tunisian bank's administrative sources.

After finishing his conversation with Professor Wilkinson, Pierre bid him goodbye and checked his watch—he was running half an hour behind.

Just a block into his fast bicycle, he heard a loud truck horn blaring behind him. He moved toward the curb to let the vehicle pass, but even after another block, the car didn't overtake him.

Then he saw her—Chandra—waiting for him and blowing him kisses. In that moment, he forgot every small problem he had, including the person relentlessly honking behind him.

He parked his bicycle and pulled out the chain lock. As he was rotating the key in the lock, he heard Chandra cry and saw her on the ground— the same guy from the honking car stood there with a handkerchief in one hand and a baseball bat in the other.

Pierre ran toward the fallen Chandra, calling Abhi as he sprinted. Just as Pierre reached the spot and was about to question the man from the honking car, the man pushed him onto the road, where a car struck him. Pierre blanked out, bleeding profusely. The honking car man ran away. Within minutes, paramedics arrived and declared Pierre dead.

Professor Wilkinson ran toward the scene, unaware of who had been hit. Chandra couldn't believe what she saw and fainted.

December 27, 2019, Chicago

She didn't wake up for the next twenty-four hours. When she finally did, she heard Abhi speaking on the phone. She couldn't focus, couldn't speak—she just closed her eyes and went back to sleep in the hospital bed.

There was a garden not far from the university. It had always been Chandra's refuge whenever academic life threatened to drain her spirit. She sat there now, on the wooden bench made of fading mahogany, the scent of greenery and roses filling her lungs. Birds chirped in the distance. Someone touched her shoulder. She knew that hand—the softness of that hairy, milky hand, its skin the color of vanilla and cream.

"Shandra…"

Those words floated to her ears, butterflies circling her

head as the wind kissed her cheek. She blushed, the pink hue spreading across her face as tracks of silver formed, tears balling down her now-red cheeks. Yet, she was smiling—a smile that came with a resounding truth. She turned to gaze into the eyes of the one she loved, the one whose hand had touched her, the one who called her name with an accent that seemed misplaced yet beautiful. But when she turned, he was... he was gone. Pierre was gone.

While Chandra was still in slumber, her mother called. The investigation into Pierre's accident had uncovered new evidence suggesting that it was not a mere accident—it was a planned homicide.

"They think Pierre could have survived the accident since he was alert and swerved. The pickup truck followed him after he escaped the first time a few weeks ago and hit him from behind—he wouldn't have been hit if he'd had a group of students with him."

"What... wait a second... why was he being chased?" Chandra asked. "It's strange that someone wanted to kill him—he was the nicest guy, and he never told me about any problems. Did it have to do with the bank irregularities he tried exposing?"

The levees had finally been compromised, shattering all the plans that had taken years to form. Tears welled up in Chandra's eyes. She broke down and started crying.

* * *

December 26, 2019, Chicago

The smell of rotten food hung heavy in the air, oozing from a garbage can just by the door. The room was a cramped one in the suburbs, but it served its purpose for the private investigator perched at a desk, scratching a few words on a pad while holding an audio recorder to his ear.

The past few weeks had been rough for Ross. He'd been chasing leads on the Anurag Roy case, all of which screamed caution with blaring red lines and warnings to keep off. But Ross had a duty—not just to his friend, Karan, but also to his own insistent curiosity about every detail of the disappearance. It was a feeling that had rooted itself from the moment he took on Karan's case. Ross clapped his hands over his face, a half-filled bottle of whiskey beside him. This was definitely going to be his last case; he was sure of it.

The day he called the Chicago taxi company—just minutes after Karan informed him about the case—Ross had lost his office. Someone had planted a bomb right under his nose. Strangely, they had left an email informing him about it. At first, Ross had dismissed it as a bad joke, but his instincts were sharp. He had leaped out of the complex just in time to watch his entire life's work erupt in orange flames. His knees weakened, a tired, awkward smile crept onto his face. That was when he knew there was a lot more to this case. It was devastating—so much so that he had called Karan the same day, saying he was backing off. Karan had warned him to play it safe, haunted by dreams of fake diamonds.

But Ross was already too deep, genuinely invested. He suspected whoever was behind this had tabs on him—his apartment, his phone line, his truck, everything. So, it made sense to play the part of a scared professional. Karan hadn't caught on yet, but with the stacks of data Ross was compiling, he was certain it would be enough to expose the truth. Fortunately, Owen—aka Luke Owens—had given him a hint.

Ross leaned back, gazing into a mirror, his badly patched face coming into view. In all his career, Ross never stopped being amazed that the least threatening people often had the makeup of creative destroyers. Owen wasn't someone who enjoyed deception, Ross thought, studying his scarred face in the reflection. Just a few more inches, and he would've lost an eye.

He refocused on the voice of a sober Owen on his audio recorder. These were Owen's last words before their fight—he had been recounting an incident from the turn of the twenty-first century.

Owen had come clean about his identity. His real name was Luke Owens, a former taxi driver for the Chicago Taxi Company. Just an ordinary guy who liked driving tourists around Chicago's architectural sites. There were two reasons for this. First, driving was the only useful skill he had. Second, he wasn't particularly social—he was awkward and had some violent tendencies that people often overlooked.

"So it's a few days before the new year, December nineteen-ninety-nine..." Owen explained. "I walk up to my taxi cab, and what do I find? A suitcase stashed with Benjamins. Tons of them. Some rich bastard forgot his money in my cab. Got so scared when I saw it—bundles of hundred-dollar bills. God, I was gonna have a heart attack."

Feeling unsafe, Owen had kept quiet about the briefcase. Reporting it to the taxi company could mean getting fired, especially if the owner filed a complaint. Each day, he bit his nails, waiting for the call that would end his career. But it never came. He began dreaming of running off with the cash when he got a strange call.

"The caller said, 'I'll tell the cops you're holding counterfeit money—you're gonna rot in jail,' stuff like that. I got scared. I didn't wanna go to jail. So, I was gonna burn the cash—burn it in my yard and just hope nobody reported the missing suitcase, 'cause I'd be toast."

But Owen didn't go through with it because the anonymous caller reached out again, this time proposing a truce. They wanted to meet, but Owen wasn't ready for that.

"But then he said, 'How would you like to make some real cash, Owen?' and I was thinking, I don't wanna get into no trouble," Owen's voice continued through the speaker of the audio recorder. "And he said, 'Well, you don't have a choice—or would you like to get fired?' That's when I knew I was screwed."

Eventually, Owen explained how he met a man at a high-class hotel. The guy had a job for him—something "simple." He had to pick up an Indian scientist, attach a chip to his taxi's number plate to block cameras from capturing it, and drop the scientist at a location. If he complied, he'd be paid a lot of money. If he contacted the cops, he'd be dead. After a few sleepless nights, Owen took the job.

Ross kept replaying a part of the recording where Owen described the hotel where he met the guy. Unfortunately, Owen never went into much detail about the man's appearance or his name. Ross also paid close attention to the area where Owen was told to drop the Indian. Owen described a kidnapping — a few men appeared out of nowhere in the alley where he had parked. No one had warned him about this. Without a word, the men dragged the Indian into a vehicle, and one of them tossed a suitcase at Owen, telling him to leave. Owen drove off before checking the suitcase.

"I opened the suitcase, and there I saw them... diamonds!" Owen's voice cried. "It was stacked with diamonds. I ran... like mad, out of Chicago. I was certain I had made it. I was rich, famous."

Owen had changed his name, fleeing with the taxi, convinced he could start a new life somewhere peaceful with the diamond money. But when he tried to sell the diamonds, the shocking truth emerged.

"The diamonds… they were fakes."

Ross had tried to stifle his laughter when he heard Owen's rant that day. Now, though, something else piqued his interest. It wasn't the hotel or the identity of the man who summoned Owen — it was something scandalous to the untrained eye but crucial to the case for Ross.

He glanced at his patched face in the mirror. To his dismay, he would have to visit Owen again. Ross called a few times, but Owen didn't pick up.

After about an hour, a text came through:

"Not in Cairo today. Had to pick someone from U Chicago — couldn't! Such bad luck."

* * *

December 28, 2019, Chicago

"Are you sure?"

"I'm fine, Mom, trust me," Chandra said to Sumati.

Of course, she was embarrassed. Being stuck in a wheelchair was never something she imagined. It was a double blow for a bubbly girl like herself, who had spent most of her college years buried behind thick academic texts, insulating herself from social life.

When the time finally came to be herself and make friends, this was what she got instead. No wonder Pierre had charmed her — she had no other life outside the confines of academia. Pierre had approached her at the library and asked her out. No drama — Chandra had almost fallen off her chair in surprise. Somehow, the two began hanging out, and word quickly spread that they were dating.

Chandra kept staring at a photo of Pierre. He had been helping her with her dissertation. Now, she had lost Pierre to an accident, broken her spine, and was doomed to a wheelchair for life — and her mom was asking if she was fine!

"No, my darling, don't cry..." Sumati hugged her.

"I... I don't know if I can do this, Mom..."

"Yes, you can, my child."

"I feel... I feel miserable... Pierre is gone, Mom. He's gone, and it's..." Her voice trailed off.

"It's all my fault."

"You're being too hard on yourself, Chandra."

"No, no, I'm not... If I had just been patient... if I hadn't insisted, we could have met elsewhere. This wouldn't have happened... it's my fault."

"You're being too hard," her mom dabbed her tears. "I don't think he would want you blaming yourself to death."

Chandra threw her arms around her mother's waist, her tear-stained face buried against her, clutching Pierre's photo tightly.

"I screwed up... I really screwed up..."

* * *

Chandra was awfully close to her father. As the only daughter, she had a right to her father that nobody else in the household had. Every month, Chandra accompanied her father to Tarapith, where her grandmother—Anurag's mother—lived. Anurag's mother often invited spiritual leaders, tantriks, and religious scholars for religious discourses and spiritual discussions.

Anurag was exposed to that environment as a child, and so was Chandra. Bama Khepa, one of the founding priests of the Tarapith temple, was believed to communicate with God. The temple was close to a cremation ground, and it was there that Bama Khepa reportedly saw God for the first time.

Anurag had a deep interest in spirituality. He was drawn to tantric philosophies and later developed a fascination with Mayan culture. He traveled to Guatemala, studied their beliefs, and met practicing individuals. In his younger days, he had also learned about out-of-body meditation.

A road tragedy took Chandra's grandmother away from her. Chandra loved her so much that she cried continuously for two days after her grandmother's death. During those days, she experienced something strange—an indescribable power.

* * *

Chandra never really had the chance to think about her gift. Pierre's death had been all too sudden, and she could never get over it. She was so shaken that she wasn't even sure she could face him in the picture world. What would she say to him? What?

Since age four, Chandra knew she was different. She had discovered her ability to communicate with people in photos. Like Karan, she too had been granted an unusual gift. It all began after her grandmother's burial. She was six then and had gone into her grandmother's old room to take another long look at the family album. She couldn't stop staring at her grandmother's photo. The reality that they had scattered her ashes in the Ganges earlier that day never stopped bothering little Chandra.

She had been staring at the photo for a long while when she suddenly felt as if she was sucked into it. And there she saw her grandmother—talking to her! But something was off—something.

Everything was frozen. Her grandmother was speaking, but nothing moved. It was like staring at a statue with a speaker tucked inside. It was strange, but Chandra kept watching. She moved closer to touch, and that was when she saw something.

Her grandmother had been saying something when, suddenly, colors began to bleed into the black-and-white world. Just as her grandmother started to move, Chandra was pulled out of the world.

Chandra had told her mom about the weird experience. At first, she thought it was just a dream, but when it happened a few more times, she feared something was wrong with her. Her mom didn't believe her until she learned that Karan also had the gift of dreaming. Chandra was both shocked and excited — her brother had powers! Her family had powers, she kept saying, jumping around. She had tormented Karan and Abhi in her bouts of excitement, imagining how cool it would be to show off her skills to friends. Abhi would usually laugh whenever she had these moments of child-like joy.

Their mother had mentioned that their father had abilities too, though she never went into specifics. Sumati never liked to talk about his disappearance, and it was always difficult to bring up the topic.

Chandra held on to Pierre's photo while her mother made dinner. In the photo, Pierre was staring at something outside the frame — a side shot. He hadn't even been smiling when it was taken.

"Why, Pierre... why did you go?"

Pierre kept glaring back, his face filling the photo frame.

"You couldn't even say goodbye, my love. Why did you have to leave... so soon?"

"I lahve yuu, Shandra."

"Me too," Chandra said, "but you promised... you promised we'd be together. We said we'd never leave each other."

"I vish ve had moore tyme... I'm sorry..."

Chandra sniffed. "I'm sorry, Pierre."

"Eetz eetz ok... I lahve yuu."

Chandra felt his hands on hers, colors bleeding out of the room, a strange wind blowing her hair. He was there with her. There. And then, he was gone.

She looked down, her eyes moist. What had just happened? Did she imagine it? That conversation felt so real. She was still clutching Pierre's photo. Had he really spoken to her? Was it just a daydream? His hands... she had felt his hands on hers. Holding the photo to her chest, fresh tears welled up in her eyes.

* * *

December 28, 2019, Chicago

"Alright, Mom. Take care."

"Alright, son. Bye."

"Bye."

Karan hung up, loosening his tie. Priya wasn't home tonight, and he could barely wait for dinner. Mom was staying with Abhi this time, and she hadn't heard from Abhi all day and was starting to worry. Before WhatsApp, this wouldn't have been a big deal — Abhi used to call her once a week using a calling card. But now, with WiFi calling, expectations had changed. Karan had assured Mom it was probably nothing to worry about.

After finishing his homemade dinner, Karan jumped into bed. He was glad to have the master bedroom all to himself, even if just for a night. He had been sleeping on the couch for weeks, and his neck was starting to ache. Priya's absence tonight made him feel even more at ease.

Karan slept early.

Chapter 10

December 29, 2019, Chicago

There was a knock on a metal door.

"Who's it?"

"Abhi? Are you there?"

The door creaked open, and a pair of eyes glared out from the darkness.

"What're you doing here?"

"Goodness, Abhi, where have you been? Everyone's worried sick... called the office—"

"What do you want, Karan?"

"Can I at least come in?"

Karan was ushered into the cramped space. There wasn't much around — just a mattress on the floor, stacks of clothes, toothpaste, a few shoes, and a small kitchen that could really use some care. Karan wasn't sure what to say.

"You shouldn't be here, Karan. I was going to call you," Abhi said, disappearing into the kitchen where a kettle was boiling.

"What was I supposed to do? You just disappeared… my apologies if we didn't discuss the finger-in-the-box incident — I thought someone was playing you... not a better time to f* with someone. Mom has been worried sick. And Chandra..."

"How's Chandra?"

"She's... she's fine — why are you here, Abhi? Why this place?"

"It's the only place where they can't find me," Abhi called from the kitchen.

"They?"

Abhi strode out, two mugs in hand. He handed one to Karan, who initially declined, but Abhi's stern gaze made him accept.

"You haven't been reading the newspaper at all?"

"Not often."

Abhi sipped his drink and handed Karan an old newspaper. "Page six."

Karan flipped to the page and stopped. He looked at Abhi, then back at the paper.

"You didn't do this."

"Tell that to the cops. There's been a manhunt. They've been looking all over for me. I'm..." Abhi gasped, "I'm now a fugitive."

Karan's hands shook as he read on, his eyes finally meeting Abhi's wide with disbelief. "Who gave you this newspaper? How did all of this happen?"

"You wouldn't believe me if I told you."

"I'm listening."

Abhi sighed, watching the steam rise from his mug.

From the private calls to the Welling Trade office in Delhi to the severed body part, Abhi filled Karan in on everything.

Abhi had been trying to renew his H1B visa. Lewis had asked one of his close clients, Mulligan and Shekhar, to show how we would delpoy Abhi on his projects for the next three years. When Lewis informed Abhi that his chances of continuing with the company were slim due to their inability to show the required contract work to immigration services, Abhi was flustered. He had known there were contracts, and something felt off. Still, this was a company he'd worked at for three years — he couldn't just let it fall apart. But things started to go south when, six months ago, Lewis stopped discussing the issue. When Abhi confronted him, Lewis simply told him to speak with Mulligan. That conversation didn't go well.

Eventually, Abhi learned that Lewis had a reputation for pulling stunts like this.

What made it worse was that Abhi couldn't file a report or explain to the immigration agency. Why? Because he was now a fugitive.

He never saw it coming. All along, he thought Lewis had introduced him to Mulligan to resolve the visa issue. But now, Abhi knew better — Lewis had set him up. And now, Abhi had a dead customer's middle finger in his apartment cops searching for him, and for reasons unknown to Abhi, even a drug cartel was on the lookout.

"What do you mean?"

"Lewis, he…I believe he knows something—"

"You're delusional."

"You...you don't understand. I... think he had mentioned about James at one point.. the same James with Dad…while he was on a call, and I overheard him. And he knew that I overheard."

"What Abhi? What? Let us bounce - gotta catch up with Ross, he must have heard about this."

Abhi stared at his brother and inhaled.

"He knows something about dad."

* * *

A black Mercedes roared across a bridge, the fiery, rusty sun spilling fierce orange hues along the path. Inside, a man sat behind the wheel, while another sat in the backseat. The man in the back wore a baseball cap and dark shades — not because of the weather.

"It's impossible," the driver said, glaring at the man in the shades through the rearview mirror. The man in the backseat kept his gaze on the passing landscapes. He didn't turn his face when he spoke.

"So I thought, but... I can feel it coming. I can tell it's coming."

"Have you forgotten how you staked your career on that deal and lost? You said you had a hunch. That hunch didn't take you far."

"That was different."

"Different, you say."

"I sense that you doubt me, and that's okay. But listen, I just know it. It's a feeling. A strong hunch. It's why I got off the grid."

"You got off the grid because they were looking for you. You did something dangerous."

"I was set up, okay..." The man in the baseball cap flashed a set of perfectly white teeth.

"You do know this will reflect badly on us — on the family."

"Do you think I did it?"

"I don't know what to believe anymore. Mom is saying one thing, Chandra is saying something else." The driver pulled over.

They had arrived.

It was the abandoned facility Ross had told them to meet at. Karan had dreamt about this building before, navigating its complex structure in his mind. Once prestigious, the structure now stood as a scar on the city's face — a beautiful mistake that nobody had shown love to in a long, long time.

The man with the shades got out of the vehicle while the driver quickly made a call.

"And?" the baseball cap guy asked.

"He's not picking up."

"I thought you said we were on an appointment."

"Let's get going."

They walked for a mile, the baseball cap guy following the other closely. Suddenly, he stopped.

"Wait."

"What?" the driver asked.

"Do you hear that?"

"Hear what?"

The man in the baseball cap strained to listen. His face tensed.

"Oh no, we've got to hurry," he said abruptly, breaking into a run.

"Why... what's wrong?"

"They've got him! They've got him!"

The other guy hurried after him. When they reached the first floor, they turned left twice and stopped at a door — its glass shattered recently.

"Oh no," the man with the shades whispered, pulling them off. "He's gone. He's gone."

When they both strode through the door, there was a body lying on the floor, a pool of blood oozing underneath him. It was the dead body of Ross Loffers.

Chapter 11

December 27, 2019, Chicago

It was eight o'clock in a quiet neighborhood with houses spaced so far apart you'd need to walk at least four minutes to reach the next one. Ross had abandoned his truck and taken the subway to this side of town. For six days, he'd been coming around, posing as some stray passer-by, hoping to catch Owen when he wasn't home. But it didn't seem ethical. Ross could've faked a search warrant, but he wasn't that kind of investigator. Besides, his face still ached from the last time Owen nearly bit it off.

The area wasn't entirely dark. A few streetlamps glowed, though some hadn't been serviced in a while. Ross could see Owen's house from his spot. He had studied the house for a while now and was starting to get tired. Unlike the other days when Owen would have been wandering around, drunk on whatever liquor he could manage to swipe from the stores, there was no sign of him tonight. Most people in the area had already figured out that Owen was a kleptomaniac.

Ross sat on a bench not far from the house. Owen's house was surrounded by a short, knee-high picket fence, so Ross could still see any movement inside. Tonight, there had been none. There was a car parked nearby. It had been there when Ross returned to his spot after tailing Owen for his usual liquor run. Ross had tried to get the license plate number when the front door creaked open.

Owen stumbled out and began to vomit intensely. When he finally staggered back inside, Ross lost interest in the car, focusing instead on Owen — waiting for the moment when the man would drink himself into a deep sleep.

The time was 9:41, and there was still no movement. Ross decided to take the risk and head to the backyard. He had reached the fence when he suddenly ducked, burying his face in the dirt. The front door had opened, and someone raced to the car, which roared to life and sped down the road.

Ross lifted his head when he was certain no one was there. He gazed at the spot where the car had been, then back at the front door—it was wide open. He looked again in the direction the car had vanished, wondering if he had seen correctly. Had it been Owen? He wasn't sure. It was possible.

Ross carefully followed the path Owen had led him through the other day. Soon, he was in the yard, spotting the patch of soil Owen had dug up to show off the diamonds. Only now did Ross realize he needed a shovel. He frowned at the thought.

He crept back to the front door, his heart pounding as he peered inside. There was no sign of life. He glanced around before stepping in.

The floor was littered with piles of bottles labeled with various brands of rum and gin. Ross minimized his steps, careful not to make a sound in case someone was inside, asleep or hiding. But the house seemed empty. All he saw were books, newspapers, and a sink filled with recently washed dishes.

As he moved toward what looked like a basement, he spotted a shattered glass of rum. Nearby, he found pictures of Luke's family—one stood out in particular. It was a photo of two men, with the caption: "Luke and Lewis – the Owens Power."

He also found some notes and documents, one with a bookmark that caught his eye. What he read compelled him to start writing in his diary:

"In 1996, Anurag had come to the Bay Area, where he met Ajit. Ajit wanted to invest in parapsychological studies on consumer behavior and use them to track price fluctuations. They were working on designing an associative remote viewing process, attempting to bypass rational consciousness and let the subconscious do most of the work subliminally. James, another researcher, was fascinated by Anurag's experiments with astral projection and other out-of-body experiences. Anurag had spoken about his learnings at Tarapith. Also, Luke's brother, Lewis, was a good friend of James."

Ross took a deep breath, his face growing increasingly pale. Ahead, he spotted a shovel. He hurriedly grabbed it and turned to leave—then he saw it.

The mouth of the shovel was moist. Ross held it closer to his face. What stared back at him made his stomach drop. Blood. Human blood mixed with sand.

A few minutes later, he found Owen's head buried in the backyard.

* * *

December 29, 2019, Chicago

Not too far away, outside the abandoned facility with a Mercedes parked in front, a man was straddled on the floor, his focus locked through the lenses of his telescopic rifle. His hair was red, and burn scars lined the left side of his face. He spoke into a Bluetooth device.

"I have them in sight."

The man on the other end had given him strict orders. Though they had never met, he had grown used to the man's voice—especially the strange texts and bank notifications. Every time, just seconds before the man called, he would receive a message and a deposit alert. No friendly chat. No backstory. Pure business. That was how he always knew a call was coming from his generous benefactor.

"Don, do not let them out of your sight. Incapacitate them if necessary."

"Roger that."

The line went dead.

This was the part of the job Don liked best. He didn't even have to waste a bullet—just had to put the fear of God into these two dust bags. He kept his sights on them.

Incapacitate them, huh?

Don panned away from the two men and focused on their car—a Mercedes. He grinned as he zoomed in on the tire.

Twip!

A soft hiss wiped out of the tyre, and soon, the car seemed out of balance as one of its tyres deflated. Knowing they might have a spare, Don fired at another tyre and the silenced bullet of his sniper lost its itself into the car's other rear tyre. He grinned contentedly. Now, he just had to wait for the strike team. These guys weren't going anywhere.

* * *

Abhi removed his baseball cap and squatted, deep in thought about the card they had been handed. Karan was still in shock.

"He must've been pretty close to you," Abhi said, staring at Ross's body.

Karan paced around, his face buried in his palm.

"Someone knew we were coming… someone knew we were going to be here."

"Now, calm down. Who else knows about this arrangement?"

"Just you. Didn't even mention it to Priya," Karan said, his voice rough. He still couldn't believe that was his friend lying there, motionless.

"We've gotta inform the cops," Karan finally declared.

"We can't."

Karan tilted his head and nodded slowly. Of course, they couldn't. Abhi would get implicated. Besides, Karan wasn't sure he could trust any investigator—not after what they had gone through with their dad's disappearance. Not after discovering the bias in the system.

But then, who would order Ross killed? He might have been a bit of an act, but he seemed like a great guy. Karan's mind raced back to what Abhi had mentioned earlier.

Could it be?

"In his diary he mentions of a Lewis. Do you think Lewis is behind this?" Abhi asked.

"I… I can't say…"

"You said he set you up, right?"

Abhi nodded, wondering where this was heading.

"You also said he knows about Dad."

Abhi's eyes brightened. Karan was now certain that Abhi knew something.

"Wait… how did you know…?" Karan strode toward his brother.

"Know what?"

"How did you know they were going to kill him? You said we should hurry. You knew. How?"

"I… I don't know, it was just a hunch," Abhi said, looking around. "Like I said back in the car, I've been having these strange remote viewing visions. They feel strong."

"Can we track Lewis? Where does he stay?"

"I don't know if that's a good idea—arggh!"

"What's wrong?" Karan dashed to his brother. Abhi had clutched his head as if a thunderbolt had struck him.

"Are you alright…?"

"We've… we've gotta call Mom…"

"Why… what's up?"

"They're in danger."

Chapter 12

December 29, 2019, Chicago

The house was quiet.

Chandra was in her room, her phone on flight mode as she went over a pre-recorded lecture. Her presentation was in a few days, and she had carefully chosen a time when she would be less distracted. Mom had gone to the market to get some groceries, leaving Chandra home alone. Her ears were plugged as she listened to her professor. She never noticed when the window slid open.

* * *

Sumati ran through the list of items she planned to purchase. She had never liked supermarkets. Back in Delhi, she preferred the organic farmers' markets, where local growers manned the stalls. She couldn't tolerate anything that compromised the quality of her food.

She frowned as she pushed her trolley past a sea of carrots, perfectly lined.

She wished she were back in Delhi, living her solo life. News of a coronavirus outbreak had been coming in from her friends in Singapore and Delhi—they had warned her not to fly. But then, her daughter needed her the most right now.

Sumati kept walking past rows and rows of items, her mask on.

"Are you looking for something specific?" A female attendant walked up to her.

"I'm sure none of this is organic," Sumati said.

The attendant beamed a smile, revealing a missing tooth. "We try to do our best."

"You wouldn't happen to know where I can get really fresh items around here?"

"We do have an organic corner—slightly expensive, but they're really fresh..."

Seeing Sumati's lack of response, she continued, "I know a local store where you can buy homegrown produce. A lot of housewives go there and complain, but of course, the store can't do anything about it. We can't either..."

"And why are you telling me this?"

The attendant stopped smiling, her expression turning more serious. "I'm sorry. I thought I'd be of help..." She turned to leave.

"No, wait..." Sumati called after her. "I'm sorry."

The woman nodded, then pointed at a man who looked like the manager.

"I thought you wanted to help!"

The girl stopped in her tracks and turned around, a slim grin spreading across her face.

"Let me come back in two minutes—just wait here, okay?"

* * *

Later that evening, Chandra sat staring at a picture of Pierre from their vacation. Sleep crept up on her, and for a moment, she felt as if she were back on that trip. In the memory, she had asked Pierre about his New Year's plans.

He had told her he wanted to visit his parents in Paris and see his niece before she started elementary school. He had also wanted Chandra to come along.

"When are you planning to come back?" she had asked. "I've invited some friends over next week."

"My visit will be a quick one. If I start early, I can come back sooner." Pierre had scribbled dates on a piece of paper. "See if these work for you."

As he handed her the card, she had folded it and slipped it into her pocket.

Now, back in the present, Chandra reached into that same pocket and pulled out a different photo—the one Abhi had given her last weekend. She frowned. Had she dreamed the whole thing? Why did it feel so real? She tried to shake herself awake, but she couldn't.

Her phone slipped from her hands. She had been holding a picture of Dad. Mom had asked her to put away Pierre's photo, and for the last several hours, she had stuck to that discipline.

Now, she was staring into Dad's eyes. She wanted to talk to him, hear his voice.

Chandra clutched the frame tightly and focused on his gaze. She imagined him speaking to her. She concentrated harder, waiting to feel…

Nothing.

That was strange.

She tried again, focusing with all her might. But nothing happened. She couldn't get pulled into the picture. It was as if some sort of barrier was blocking her.

She tried harder… and harder.

Nothing.

It was strange. This was the first time she had tried to talk to Dad since her accident. The last time had been a long time ago.

Although Mom was against it, Chandra had secretly attempted it when Mom wasn't watching—but she still couldn't enter the picture.

Over the past year, she had tried to enter photos of friends and important people, but it never worked. She quickly realized that her ability only functioned when she stared at photos of people who were no longer alive. The discovery had puzzled her at first, but she eventually convinced herself that she was some sort of clairvoyant. The idea terrified her so much that she threw away all the photos of deceased people she owned.

During lectures, whenever a photo of a late philosopher or scientist appeared on the projector, she shut her eyes. Since she didn't recognize most of them by face, she memorized their names instead—just to be safe.

Now, Chandra still clutched her father's photo.

Why couldn't she access him now? Why?

She longed to hear his voice, hoping he might have something to say about the presentation she was preparing.

Why was this happening to her?

And why now?

Wait.

She shook her head and stared at the photo again. Something felt off.

She racked her brain, trying to figure out what it was. She knew something—something important—but she couldn't remember what.

Suddenly, she raced to her diary, nearly toppling off her wheelchair. She flipped through the pages frantically, running her fingers over them until she found it.

Her heart sank as she read the entry aloud.

It wasn't anything specific—just a note from the day she discovered the limits of her powers. If she could only communicate with the dead, then the fact that she could no longer access her father's voice meant one thing. Just one thing.

Her dad was al—

Chandra stopped mid-thought.

What was that?

Her eyes darted to the open window. She was certain she had locked it earlier.

She wheeled herself closer, straining to look outside. She leaned as far forward as she could, just enough to see the lawn.

Her breath hitched. She fell back onto her wheelchair, nearly losing her balance. Her heart was pounding wildly as she scrambled upright and reached for her phone.

She had to call Mom. She had to call her right now.

Because on the lawn, she had seen something.

Two footprints.

Someone had climbed through the window.

She reached for her phone, dialing Mom's number.

The call failed. A notification popped up, reminding her that flight mode was still on.

Chandra cursed, fumbling to turn it off. In her haste, the phone slipped from her grasp and hit the floor with a dull thud.

"Damn it!" she hissed, dropping to the ground. She crawled on her elbows, the rough surface of her polished floor scraping against her skin. She winced, cursing herself for spending her entire savings on such impractical décor. Her elbows burned, but she pushed forward, reaching for the phone.

Just as she grasped it, the screen lit up. An incoming call.

"Abhi!" she gasped, answering instantly.

"Chandra!"

"Abhi, thank God! Someone's inside! I saw it—I saw it—someone's in the house!"

"Chandra, get out! Now! It's not safe at home!"

"I know, I know—God, help me... Mom... Mom's not home?"

"What?"

"I'm alone—someone's in the hous—"

Smack!

Something forceful struck Chandra in the face, causing her to fall forward. Her phone clattered as it hit the floor somewhere out of reach. She winced and tried to get up...but couldn't.

She heard pounding footsteps drawing closer and the sound of metal scraping against the floor. She looked up through her foggy vision—her wheelchair. Whoever it was had thrown it far from her grasp.

Her view was blurry. Someone was crouched above her now, a face hidden behind a mask. She tried to move, but something cold pressed against her neck.

"Don't move," the voice said as a needle pierced her skin, flooding her system with an ice-cold fluid. Her vision blurred further, her body growing heavy. Darkness pulled at her.

"Please...please, don't... hurt m..."

She drifted into unconsciousness.

The masked man checked her pulse. She was out. The injection would keep her under for about an hour—enough time before the van arrived.

He pressed a device in his ear. A voice crackled to life.

"I've got her."

* * *

"What happened?"

"I don't know, the line went off... she was saying something." Karan said, making a right turn with Abhi on his tail.

Soon, they were bathed in sunlight, the Mercedes a few yards away.

"Where is she?"

"She should be home… with Mom."

"Alright—"

Bang! Bang!

A couple of shots perforated the moonroof of the Mercedes. Abhi yanked Karan's arm as shattered glass rained down. The car alarm blared.

"Hurry." Abhi pulled his brother back into the building. Karan was breathing heavily when they got inside.

"Are you okay, man?" Abhi asked.

Karan nodded hesitantly, staring back at his car. There might have been a bomb.

"There's gotta be a back door."

"Wait. I've got a plan."

* * *

Don remained hidden from view behind a window on the top floor of the building. He was smoking a joint when he spotted one of the two men he had fired at—the one in plain clothes. His name was supposed to be Karan.

Don sat up for an unobstructed view. Karan was walking out of the building slowly, both hands in the air.

Don's brows arched.

He's surrendering?

He laughed, wondering just what these guys were thinking. Peering into the camera hole of his sniper, he scanned the area. He had a pretty good idea of what they were up to.

Some ploy to distract me so they can make a run for it.

Not happening.

The sad thing was that the entire building was a literal prison yard. It was completely sealed—no back door, no shortcuts. Just a massive, dead structure built for corporate slaves who once graced its floors half a century ago. The windows were barred with iron. The perimeter was fenced with thick brick and metal.

They were joking if they thought they could play games with him.

Don picked up his earpiece from the windowsill, where bits of ash lay. He hesitated before tucking it into his ear. Did he really need to report this?

He shrugged and hit the dial.

Seconds later, a familiar, delusional voice greeted him.

"Any improvements?" the voice on the other end rang.

"Yes, they appear to have come up..." Don sniffed as he spoke, "with some plan... one of them is currently outside, hands in the air."

"Have you been smoking, Don?"

Don's face went pale. He scratched his head. "No, how can I...? This is important work."

"I'm glad you understand. There are two of them— is the other one outside as well?"

"No, no, the other one is still inside. It's just... just this one. Do you want me to check him out?"

"That's hardly important now. Just hold your position. The strike team will be there soon. You'll be their eyes up there."

"Alright."

"Just try not to lose them."

"Roger that."

Don stubbed out the joint as he ended the call, his gaze locking onto the man—

Uh-oh!

Don cursed. The man was gone.

His eyes scanned the area through the binoculars.

"Damn it!" Don hissed, tucking his pistol into his belt as he unmounted his tools from the window.

If this guy got away, he was as good as dead. And then there was the other one—heaven knows what he was up to.

Don looked around, trying to gather his thoughts, but his head was a mess. Damn it. He shouldn't have smoked that joint. Not now. He couldn't stay put. He had to move. With a groan, he marched out the door with killer precision. These guys were in for a hell of a time, he cursed, cocking his gun as he disappeared into the hallway.

* * *

Karan took a deep breath. He wasn't sure if the shooter had really left his spot on the top floor or was just taking a break. Whatever the case, he was sweating. Sweating big time. He remained where he was, hidden in his now-damaged Mercedes, just as Abhi had instructed. His mind raced, considering what he was about to do—and how it would implicate his brother. Before he stepped out, Abhi had given him strict instructions. Instructions that had left his jaw slack.

"Are you sure about this?" Karan had asked after Abhi explained the plan.

"You'll have to trust me on this, brother."

"And you can sense all this... from a hunch?"

Abhi nodded.

Karan had thrown an arm around his brother. He wasn't sure what was going to happen. If they got caught, or if—by some stroke of bad luck—he got killed, he couldn't imagine what Abhi would do. He may have always come off as cold to his brother, but he...

"Are you listening?" Abhi's voice snapped him back.

Karan shook his head. "Wait... what? You were saying?"

"I said you better hurry. Remember—nice and slow. We don't want to pressure him into taking a shot."

Karan nodded, took a deep breath, raised his hands, and started walking toward the entrance.

He wasn't sure he fully understood Abhi's plan, but he wasn't about to ask. That wasn't how Abhi worked. As much as Karan hated his guts sometimes, his brother was smart.

However, their values were different. Where Karan cherished security, Abhi thrived on risk and near-death calls.

Well, he thought, I hope you're right about this, Abhi.

With that, he took out his cell phone…

And dialled 911.

Chapter 13

Don was jumping flights of stairs, his eyes darting everywhere as adrenaline surged through his system. He was high. High on the stimulant he had smoked just moments ago. Everything around him seemed dull, like the world was in slow motion. His mouth hung open like a junkie's—like a dog's—like someone who had lost a vital part of himself. His soul. The very thing that made him who he was.

His eyes were hellholes. Reddish. Hellish. Demons burned in them alongside a thousand saints and a thousand frauds. Demons. Thoughts. Burning. Eternal burning. Fire. Screams. Blood. Rage.

Rage.

That was it, Don realized. He wasn't just angry—he was enraged. These two bastards were about to screw up his deal. Damn right, he had every reason to be furious. He had to be.

He jumped another set of stairs, landing with military precision. His hands were spread out, his gun tucked between them, ready to explode into anyone—anything—that crossed his path. He ran, fueled by all the fury in the world. Every ounce of pent-up anger his chaotic mind could muster was now unleashed.

Don had raced through a series of doors when he suddenly stopped.

Creeeaaaaakkkk.

A door creaked somewhere nearby. He turned around, mind stretched to its limit, waiting—waiting for that one sound that would give away someone's presence. Someone who would become the victim of his bottled-up rage.

In that moment, he had no concept of right or wrong. He didn't care that he had been specifically instructed *not* to kill anyone. He just wanted relief. He wanted to feel *better*. He wanted to *climax* at the sight of blood exploding. At the sound of someone's scream. He wanted to do it. And do it fast. Leaning against the wall, he walked slowly now. Listening.

Scratch. Scratch. Scratch.

There was movement. Movement on the other side. Someone was in there.

With a broad grin, Don raced into the room, squeezing the trigger.

Fritzzz!

An electric pulse shot from his gun, losing itself in a blank wall, sending a flock of doves flying. Don stared at the empty room—and laughed.

"Of course," he muttered, remembering that he had left his pistol back at the van, afraid that his killer instincts would take over mid-mission. He couldn't jeopardize everything, could he? It was a wise decision, he thought, strolling over to where the dart from his taser lay.

He glanced out the window at the junkyard below, filled with the carcasses of machines long forgotten. There was definitely no one in the room. Just birds messing around. And the thought of it made his chest tighten. The boss wouldn't like this.

With a click, the teaser was turned off, and Don tucked the weapon back into his belt. He leaned forward, staring through the steel window bars. The junkyard spread out before him, filled with trucks—lines and lines of white trucks with rusting containers on their backs. Scattered throughout were worn-out industrial gears, treadmills, exposed engines, wrecked automobiles, and bulldozers, all gathering dust and moths.

Don looked around and noticed one of the trucks had its container wide open. The entrance had just moved. He frowned, knowing his guy was hiding in there. He raced for the door.

Don barely made it out when something hard slammed into his face. For a moment, he felt weightless as the world spiraled and the ground rushed up to meet him.

Thud!

His head kept spinning. Damned marijuana, he thought, glaring at the man who had struck him. Standing before him was the second man—the one with the jacket and baseball cap. He was holding something. A spanner.

Don felt wetness on his nose. When he ran his fingers along the contours of his face, he was met with crumpled flesh. His hand shook as he felt it.

"My nose… you freaking broke my nose!" Don gasped, staring at the red fluid soaking his hand.

He pulled out the teaser and fired, but the man had vanished. Don leaped to his feet—then a gut-wrenching pain tore through his kneecaps, the sound of bones shattering. He grabbed at the man's jacket, shoving the barrel of his gun into his chest.

Frrrzz!

Abhi yelped as a nerve-wracking sensation tore through his body. As a blue surge covered him, he threw his arms around the bulky man, and soon, both of them were writhing in agony.

Seconds later, a bloody hand clamped down hard on his throat. Abhi coughed, wiggling under those strong claws. The hands didn't budge.

"You're gonna bleed, you hear that?" Don said as Abhi's face turned red. Abhi clawed at the floor and threw a handful of sand into the man's face.

"Fu—" The man cursed, his grip loosening as he stumbled backward.

Abhi lunged in that instant, throwing his weight into the man's chest before grabbing the spanner.

Bwack!

The man groaned as he collapsed onto all fours, his knees shuddering beneath him. Abhi had struck his kneecaps. The man kept groaning, his face red like the color of his hair. Then, he started laughing—laughing like some dead-ass Joker.

"We're gonna kill them… you hear that?" the man said. "The woman… the girl… we're gonna kill them after we've harvested your powers. And then, I'll be seeing you in hell."

Abhi's heartbeat pounded. He was talking about Sumati and Chandra. He stepped closer, blood dripping from his upper lip.

"Where are they?" Abhi demanded.

The man grinned and raised his middle finger.

"You can shove it down your ass—"

"Arrrgghhhh!" the man groaned.

Don yelped, veins protruding from his neck as he clutched his finger. The bastard had broken it. He gritted his teeth, his eyes flaring as he imagined all the violent things he would do to this guy.

"Is…" Don said through clenched teeth, "is that the best… you've got…?"

"I really don't want to do this," Abhi said.

"Well, it's too late for sissy talk. You and your… your lil' family. You're already dead. Ahah, dead."

Abhi saw the spanner swinging hard at him. He ducked just in time. Don groaned, flustered. In the next instant, Abhi grabbed both his legs and shoved him forward, toppling him backward.

Then the hits came.

Bwack. Bwack. Bwack.

Abhi and Don hammered out punches, fists flying. There was no thinking. Don just wanted to destroy this face—this evil, ugly face. He kept punching. He didn't even realize when Abhi had slipped out from under him.

Don kept punching.

Two minutes later, he realized he was hitting a rag stuffed with old clothes.

Why was the rag there? Was this some site for coven experiments? Nobody knew, nor was anyone motivated to find out.

Don reached out an arm for support, trying to lift his body through the pain.

Aaaarrrrhhhh!

He had touched open wires and got electrocuted. All sorts of agony swallowed Don right there and he fell on his face, motionless.

***

Karan remained hidden in the Mercedes, his hands tapping on his thighs as sweat gathered on his palms. He could hear the distant wail of sirens growing closer. He had prayed to every god he knew that everything would be fine.

Earlier, he had heard screams. The clatter of metal crashing to the ground. Then, suddenly, everything had gone quiet again.

As he stared at the building, it looked as if everything had ended. The barred windows glared back at him like doorways to some lake of fire. His body was so drenched in sweat that the seat beneath him had started to feel mushy.

Suddenly, someone staggered out of the building.

Karan's heartbeat tripled as he saw a man approaching the Mercedes, carrying a gun. He couldn't tell who it was— the windshield was riddled with bullet holes, obscuring his view.

Panicking, Karan hurriedly tried to start the car.

Vrrr.

It didn't start. He tried again.

Nothing.

Sweat poured down his face as his shaky hands reached for the back door, preparing to run—when heavy knocks came on the scarred window.

Karan froze, hoping whoever it was would leave. Maybe it was just a stray security officer tapping at the wrecked car.

Or maybe it wasn't.

Knock knock knock.!

Karan didn't move. Suddenly, the door swung open. His heart froze in that instant.

"Why the f*ck are you motionless?!" a familiar voice bellowed.

Karan leaned forward. The moment he saw Abhi, the color returned to his face.

"Good god, you're alright!" Karan said, climbing out of the car. Abhi looked like a survivor of an atomic war—his face bruised, his head covered in dirt and blood.

"Are you alright?" Karan asked as his brother hurriedly pulled off his shirt.

"We've got to get out of here… fast," Abhi said, the sound of sirens growing louder.

Karan nodded. "Yeah… but we'll get traced if we leave now. Our prints are all over this place."

Abhi gritted his teeth, acknowledging the truth. Karan had thought everything through. Even if they managed to escape, the car was still here—enough evidence to put him in jail for life. What the hell was his car doing at a murder scene? He could already hear the tabloids and reporters screaming the headlines. But there was no time to dwell. They needed to act. Fast.

"I've got a plan, bro…" Abhi said.

"Yeah, me too."

"Alright, let's hear yours..." Abhi said, his eyes scanning the area with sharp intensity.

"I... well... I..." Karan fumbled for words, then gave up. "Look, I have no idea what we'll do. All I know is—we can't get caught. We mustn't."

"Exactly what I was thinking..."

Karan shot his brother a glare. "Really? That was your plan?"

Abhi managed a weak smile. "No... but what I have in mind... I don't think you'll like it."

Chapter 14

December 29, 2019, Chicago

The man in the face mask glanced at his watch. The van was running late.

His phone rang.

"Where the hell are you guys?"

"Sorry… there was a bit of a ruckus at the factory. We'll be there in twenty… maybe half an hour."

"And the woman?"

A pause. Then the voice returned.

"She's safe."

"Alright, see you soon."

The call disconnected.

* * *

Not far away, news spread of a store attendant drugging an elderly Indian woman, gagging her, and taking her away.

* * *

Two police cars arrived at the abandoned building. Earlier, they had been radioed about an electrocution.

A male and a female officer jumped out of their vehicles, guns drawn. They were heading toward the building when a low, persistent grunt came from a wrecked car nearby.

They hurried over, weapons ready, and yanked the door open.

Inside, Karan sat bound, his hands and feet tied. He moaned weakly.

* * *

Not far from the scene, a bright blue van had pulled over by the roadside. Inside were three men dressed in blue overalls with *House Cleaning* emblazoned across their chests. Except, their vehicle was stocked with hostile artillery. One of the men peered through a pair of binoculars, eyes locked on the crime scene.

"Hurry, phone the boss. Don's been busted," he said.

The largest of the three scrambled to pull out a device, then handed it to the guy with the binoculars.

"What?" The binoculars guy shot him a glare.

"You said you wanted to talk to the boss—"

"Call him yourself, damn it!"

The call connected. The big guy cleared his throat, his lips trembling as he spoke.

"Boss…"

"Picked them up yet?"

"Err… about that… cops… at the site…"

"Shit. Get the hell out of there! And why are you even there now? We *can't* lose the girl and the mother."

"Yes, yes, understood." He hung up and turned to the guy with the binoculars. "Next stop."

The van roared away. None of them noticed the stranger who had just hopped onto the roof.

* * *

The man with the face mask kept glaring at the clock. They were late. If he didn't wrap things up quickly, the girl would wake up. And he might have to give her another shot of the injection. He wasn't sure of the health implications, but he just couldn't have her waking up during the heist.

The doorbell rang.

The man's gaze snapped to the door. That was odd. He checked his mobile device to see if he had missed a call. There were no missed calls. If the guys were here already, they would've called.

He hurried to the window, stealing a glance for the familiar van. There was no van on the street. Just fleets of cars going here and there. Nothing familiar, no proof that his team was here for the pickup.

He tiptoed to the door, pressing his ear against it. Someone was talking. A woman.

"Hello? Chandra, are you in there? It's Stacy..."

The masked man receded into the room, certain that this Stacy would leave.

He was wrong.

Hardly had he reached the other room when the doorknob started to turn. There was the sound of a key being inserted into the lock, and soon, the door gave way.

Stacy stepped into Chandra's apartment. It was quiet. Unusually quiet. And stuffy. Had Chandra locked herself indoors?

Stacy took only a few steps before noticing that some things seemed out of order. Worse, there was no sign of Chandra. She reached for her purse, pulled out her phone, and dialed Chandra's number, wondering if she had gone out and forgotten their engagement.

Stacy needed help with her psychology class. Chandra had said she could come over anytime and had given her a set of keys. Now, here she was, and there was no Chandra.

Besides schoolwork, Stacy was an old friend of Chandra. She was drawn to Chandra's intellectual depth.

A low hum vibrated through the wooden floor. It was coming from the bedroom.

Was Chandra hurt? Had she fallen while doing chores?

Stacy walked forward cautiously, her gaze sweeping the room. Then she stopped. She had seen it. A phone lay on the floor, its screen shattered. Not too far from it lay Chandra's crumpled body.

Stacy wanted to scream. Before she could open her mouth, a hand clamped hard over it. Panic surged through her. She stomped at the intruder's feet and elbowed his groin, but he was quicker. He rammed a needle into her neck, emptying its contents into her bloodstream.

Stacy slumped to the floor. She went limp right on.

Shiz.

The masked man cursed. He had wasted his last syringe on this girl. That would pose a problem. He hoped the guys had a spare in the van.

His phone rang.

"We're outside."

"I'm waiting—"

The line went dead.

He frowned. Why had they cut the call so abruptly?

Moving to the window, he glanced down at the street. The blue cleaning van was parked just across the road. His guys.

But something was off. The van wobbled, shaking slightly, as if a circus was going on inside.

"What on earth are these guys doing?"

He pulled up the window blind and dialed again.

"What the fox? Are you dancing or what? Freaking get the hell down here."

Silence.

Then, an unusually deep voice replied, "Okay."

The masked man stared at Chandra. It was a pity that a pretty girl like her had ended up in a wheelchair. He had to dress her up—couldn't exactly carry a human being in broad daylight without attracting attention.

The door swung open. A man in overalls and a face cap hurried in.

The masked man glanced at his comrade, relieved they could finally get the hell out of here.

"Where are the others?" he asked.

"The boys aren't feeling well. Thought you might need this." The man handed him a syringe.

"Yeah, thanks." The masked man took it, nodding as he wondered how this guy had figured he needed a spare.

He crouched over the girl. The man did the same.

"What the hell was going on? I saw the van rocking," the masked man said, stretching a sheet over the girl.

"You wouldn't believe it if I told you..."

"Oh yeah?" The masked man smirked. "You're from Chicago, right? Bob?"

The man licked his lips. "Y—yeah. Bob."

"Alright." The masked man stood up. "You know something, Bob?"

"What?"

"I never met an a-hole as smart as you." He paused, grinning. "I don't know anyone called Bob."

Without hesitation, he stabbed the man with the syringe.

The man fell, his face cap slipping off.

The masked man chuckled, standing over him.

"It's nice to finally meet you in person, Abhi."

Chapter 15

December 30, 2019, Chicago

Karan was in police custody.

Since the cops had found him at the abandoned facility, they had detained him. He had been there for hours now, his eyes nearly bloodshot from the sleepless night—thanks to the constant noise and stench from the other cells.

He was waiting for his state-appointed attorney. A bank robbery was in progress, and all the cops were occupied, so he would be spending the night there.

Exhausted, he tried to connect with his mother through a dream. But he couldn't. He tried harder. Instead, he connected with someone else—someone familiar.

Karan mentioned that he had been to India and that his brother had also flown to Kolkata. The person on the other end of the dream asked, "Is Abhi your brother?"

That sheer coincidence jolted him awake. But a few hours later, that person reached out to Karan again—this time, in his dream. She told him her story—how she got into psychotropic drugs and learned lucid dreaming.

For Karan, this was the first time someone had reached out to him through dreams, so eager to connect. She shared her frustration—her brother's murderers were still at large. As their brief conversation came to an end, Karan asked her name.

She said, "Bhavna Sengupta."

* * *

He had been sitting on the hard bed, watching a fly, when an officer reached his cell.

"Someone's here to see you." The officer opened the cell and ushered Karan out.

Karan's face was musty, his hair rough. He was escorted to the visiting room. His eyes flooded with tears when he saw her.

Priya.

"My God, Karan, what have they been feeding you?"

"I'm… I'm fine," Karan said as they embraced and sat. His neck ached from sleeping on a concrete-like bed. It had been 24 hours since they picked him up from that abandoned building.

At the building, the cops had found two dead bodies—one was Ross, the other was their shooter. Karan had tried to explain, following the plan Abhi had come up with. Abhi thought it would be best if someone remained at the scene to prevent a thorough investigation. Since he was still an outlaw, Abhi was about to go to jail. With his brother's consent, Abhi tied Karan up to make him look like a kidnapping victim.

It sounded like a great plan. However, when the cops showed up, they weren't buying the story.

"Have you called the lawyer… when are they granting my bail?"

"Karan…" Priya touched his palm. "There's a bigger issue."

Karan frowned, clapping his palm over his face. He thought he knew what she was going to say—that Chandra and Sumati had been unreachable. Some part of him had glimpsed this in a dream, but he didn't know how true it was. Dreams didn't always turn out as you wanted them to. Although he could manipulate them to some degree, it was hard to tell reality from fear, especially when he already had a hint that the people in his dreams might be in danger. Dreams played on his subconscious, feeding him his deepest fears.

"What happened?" Karan asked sheepishly, touching her hand. It was soft. Soft as wool. So delicate. Was this the woman he had ignored so often? Suddenly, she looked different, and it felt good to feel the warmth of her hand on his.

"You're..." Priya stuttered. "You're facing litigation."

Karan's head spun. He hadn't heard correctly. The words echoed in his mind. Litigation. Court. Jail.

Litigation.

Karan moved his head slowly, as if someone had hit him with a club.

"What... are you saying?"

Priya inhaled, trying to regain composure. He could see she was trying to stay strong. There were dark circles under her eyes—she had been crying all night. This, he could tell. And yet, she looked charming.

Priya cleared her throat and spoke. "They are charging you with fraud."

"How's that possible?"

"Our lawyer... he says you knew about this... that it was only a matter of time before things got messy."

"I don't understand. What... what are you talking about?" Karan's voice wavered between anger and weakness.

"God, Karan, your company hires International candidates that need visas to work. Some firms that sponsor these candidates, inadvertently, use the work contract meant for one person, to sponsor another person. You might have the same problem."

Karan froze where he sat, drowning in self-denial. It wasn't true. It couldn't be true.

Yes, he had contracts. But his analytics start-up hired consultants to work on the company's own products and not sit at customer sites. So, this didn't make sense.

This was not good.

"I need to get out of here," he said.

Priya nodded. "Yes. I've been on the phone all night, calling friends and family who might know someone. So far, there's no guarantee—"

"Get me out of here!" Karan kept repeating, his voice growing louder.

Then he stopped, his eyes red with tears.

"Karan, I'll never leave your side... I'm right here," Priya said.

Karan wiped his eyes and nodded. "When can I see my lawyer... when?"

"He'll be here tomorrow."

Karan nodded as the guards stepped forward to escort him back to his cell.

"Take care, my love," she said, watching him leave.

They had taken him to the door when he suddenly turned.

"Priya..." he called out. "Priya, I love you..."

Priya smiled back. And then he was gone, vanished behind the steel door. He didn't see her cry.

* * *

December 30, 2019, Chicago

The room was dark, a dim green lamp hanging above a chair where an old man sat, chewing on an electric cigarette.

His phone rang.

"What is it?"

"We've got them..."

"Good, good... all of them, including the girl?"

"Yes, but... the first of them... the man, he's in—"

"Police custody. I know. Not to worry. Excellent job. We'll talk later."

"Alright, boss."

The man ended the call and immediately dialed another number.

"How's it going, sweetheart?"

"Not bad. How are they?"

"We got them... not all, but the important ones."

"Great. Talk about a family reunion."

"Haha, what can I say? Their gifts... quite priceless."

"How much do you think we'll get for the girl?"

"Well," the man said, "we'll have to test her first, but I suppose she'll be worth double her father."

"No way!" the voice on the line exclaimed.

"Yes."

A pause.

"Wow, I never thought so... anyway, good luck with that. I'm trying to break our next target out of police custody."

"Good luck... and remember to keep things subtle."

With that, the line went dead.

The man smiled in satisfaction.

He turned to gaze at an unusually large glass-walled apartment. Seated inside, legs folded in a meditative pose, was a man.

A man who had vanished twenty years ago.

James laughed.

Chapter 16

December 31, 2019, Chicago

Karan strolled to the front desk of the station, observing the officers on the other side of the counter. Priya and a lanky man in a suit stood next to him—Mark, his attorney.

"Sign here, please," an officer said, offering a pad.

Karan signed and followed Priya and Mark outside to a waiting car.

"Thanks, Mark," Karan said as he climbed in. "Any plans for New Year's?"

"We need to come up with a plan for your case. The jury will demand more information about the company," Mark replied.

Karan nodded, his hands wrapped around Priya's. "We'll do all that later. Right now, I just want to go home."

"Of course..." Mark said as he pulled out of the facility.

* * *

Chandra was in a black hole.

At least, that was what the place looked like when she woke to the sound of dripping water. She felt weightless, a strong tension pulling at her wrists. Shivering, the cold bit deep into her skin. Where was she? Who would want to hurt her? And why?

In the moments before she woke, she had heard a voice—like her father's. It kept repeating one thing. Just one thing.

Lies. It's all lies…

But the voice had faded the instant she woke.

"Hello?" she called out, her voice swallowed by the darkness, drowned by the steady drip, drip, drip of water. It was numbing. Her wrists ached. She looked down—and to her horror, there was no ground beneath her feet. Her stomach churned as she tilted her head upward. Her hands were bound by chains stretching into the endless black above.

"Somebody help me!" she screamed. But there was no one to help her. No one to save her. She was alone, without her wheelchair or her mother's guidance. She had been abducted.

Her abductor had worn a mask. Her brother had mentioned someone in her room. But there was something before that. Yes—she had discovered something. Something about her father. That was before she saw the open window, before she noticed the footprints on the lawn.

She screamed again. "Somebody help!"

A light flickered on from a passage ahead. Footsteps approached. She couldn't see who it was, but they kept coming. Closer. Closer.

A man. A familiar face.

He opened his mouth to speak. "We are in danger, Chandra."

Chandra gasped. She could see his face clearly now.

It was her father.

"We are in danger."

"Father—"

"Listen to me. You have to hear everything I say," Anurag said. "Chandra, my research shows that we exist in at least two worlds—let's just say two to keep it simple. When we die, we transition to the second world as entirely different beings. Then, we return to this world as someone else. But that's too much to process right now. Let's go back to bed."

Chandra hesitated. "But what about heaven and hell?"

"Not necessarily," Anurag replied. "Both worlds are good. Religion and virtue exist as guidelines to ensure people treat each other well."

Chandra couldn't change Anurag's past by stepping into the picture. But she had to remember why she was doing this—and she needed something from the present to return. So, she took a photo from the Thanksgiving party earlier that year.

"Also, Chandra, according to some cosmic physics theories, consciousness exists as an energy form," Anurag explained. "I've been working on something I call the recorded trail. It seems that everything we do is stored as actions, and these recordings replay periodically—maybe every ten years or even as little as one year."

"But, Baba, doesn't consciousness die with the body?" Chandra asked.

"Yes, Chandra, that's what most people believe. But in some cases, these recorded trails appear even while a person is still alive. Sometimes, people see themselves as if watching a real-life double, and they get scared by these lingering reflections of their past actions."

"That's so spooky, Dad!"

"I've done some work on out-of-body experiences, similar to the practices of Bama Khapa's followers in Tarapith," Anurag said. "By the way Chandra there are two scientists running tests on you - they don't know I am here so keep it that way."

Chandra nodded. Suddenly, she felt herself being lowered to the ground, where a wheelchair was waiting. The space around her was vast and completely black, with no light except for the faint glow spilling in from the pathway Anurag had walked through. Dense black glass walls surrounded her, blocking out any external light.

On the other side of the glass, two scientists observed her closely. Data streamed across multiple screens as they took notes.

"She's responding," the younger scientist said.

"Yes..."

"How long before she realizes, Dr. X?"

"It's hard to say, but her stress levels are rising."

The younger scientist nodded.

"Yes," a deep voice boomed through the lab. "It is satisfactory. How is it going with the son?"

"He's giving us a hard time."

"He's a tough one, that one," the voice responded.

Dr. X nodded, glancing at the man encased in a glass frame.

"Why do you think he rejects the program, Dr. X?" the voice asked.

"That's still a mystery. His sister seems to be adapting well."

"Yes, but how do you explain their mother? She readily believes it's him. Why?"

Dr. X turned to a monitor displaying an older woman, restrained in the same way as the girl.

"Well, it could be many things. I assume she has doubts, but she's seeing her long-lost husband after so many years. It's hard not to succumb to her emotions."

"So, you're saying she's convinced..."

"More or less, yes."

"Alright."

Dr. X switched the call to her earpods, lowering her voice to a whisper.

"May I ask why we have the woman, sir?"

"She's our bait. If things get difficult, a little motivation will make them desperate to save their own skin."

Dr. X swallowed hard, nodding slightly.

"In the meantime, commence the extraction procedure for the girl."

"I don't think it's advisable at this stage—"

"Doctor, we don't have time for ethical debates. You said it yourself—we don't know how long she'll remain in this state. We need to extract those abilities before she awakens…"

"I know, I know, but it's just not stable. I need to perfect the sedative… We don't want to destabilize her during the procedure. I'm not sure how much her brain can take—her blood pressure is already high."

"How long before you can perfect it?"

"It should only take a few days—"

"How long, Dr. X?"

Dr. X glanced at the younger scientist, who silently mouthed the word *four*.

"Four… four days…" she said.

"You have forty-eight hours, Doctor."

"But sir—"

"That would be all. Make it happen."

* * *

James got off the call with the scientist. He kept re-watching the live video of the girl. She was a beautiful Indian girl with qualities that surpassed her father's.

James glared at the chart on a wall-sized screen. Rows and columns filled the display. Above the chart were the words: EXTRACTION CUSTOMERS.

* * *

Maria Velasco was in her twenties when she met James in Manila. He was visiting his cousins and staying at a hotel in Paisag City. On their second meeting, James asked her out, using his favorite pick-up line:

"The world is a bright place today, and I think it will be brighter if you go out with me this evening."

She smiled. There was nothing wrong with going out with him. That evening was the best James had spent in a long time.

Maria's parents always wanted her to marry a Filipino man, and James fit the bill perfectly. Though he had moved to the U.S. with his parents at the age of five, they were originally from the Boracay Islands. His father had worked in the public works department in Iloilo City before deciding to relocate.

When James first arrived in the U.S., he barely spoke English. Yet, within a year, he surprised everyone by becoming fluent—a testament to how quickly he adapted. Making friends came just as easily to him. He later pursued psychology, always intending to enter academia and earn the title Dr. Barnes.

The next month, they drove through Intramuros, the historic district of Manila.

"Intramuros was built by Spanish missionaries to protect the inner city from invading pirates and civil uprisings," Maria explained, sharing the significance of Filipino architecture.

James stopped the car to take pictures. But instead of reaching for his camera, he pulled out a ring, bent down, and held it out to Maria. At first, she thought it was a joke and tried to laugh it off. But it wasn't. Then James uttered the magic words:

"Will you marry me?"

Maria felt this was it—what she had always wanted. Marrying a prince from the West. She said yes, overwhelmed with happiness since the day she met James.

But within two years of marriage, after moving to the U.S., cracks began to form in their relationship. Beyond their cultural differences, they realized the love between them had started to fade.

However, Maria could only take so much—there was no cheating, no deception, no abuse—just an agreement that there was a void in their love. James had suggested that a baby could fill the void. However, Maria did not agree—she thought it would just add to the harrowing emptiness. And how would they raise a kid together if they did not like each other, to begin with? She wanted out. She had already gotten her permanent residency in the US and would have had no trouble sustaining herself. James gradually realized that there was no chance of bringing love back. He had also started questioning whether love had ever existed between them and had begun seeing it more as a green card ploy by Maria.

James and Maria spent Valentine's Day together—all day. They discussed how they had lifted a Christmas tree at the eleventh hour when their online-ordered tree did not show up and how she had to cook food quickly when five of James's close friends decided to throw a surprise birthday party for him. They shared several other stories about the time they spent together. However, at the end of the day, they bid each other goodbye and went back to their respective apartments alone.

That was when James decided to move to Chicago to forget everything and absolve everyone. The property prices were moderate yet inviting to risk-takers, especially with offers such as "Move in today" and "Don't pay anything for the first two years." For someone who had recently been denied the hope of sustaining a happy family, this was perhaps one of the best things that could happen.

In Chicago, James continued his research on the development of the subconscious when he met Anurag through Jenny.

* * *

The extraction market was an industry that developed as an offshoot of the dark web. While the dark web dealt with the sale of illegal goods, firearms, and assassins, among other things, the extraction market focused on something far more personal. It was created for the study of gifted individuals' DNA, brain patterns, and genetic characteristics, but some turned it into an active trade in these abilities.

The extraction itself was a complicated procedure, requiring extensive preparation. To extract someone's abilities, the target had to be in a state of rest before being placed on a machine that could read their brain activity and patterns. In that state, the subject remained for a period while being shown various snippets to gauge how their brain perceived and reacted to them. These reactions, along with the brain patterns, were then sold to the highest bidder on the extraction market.

James was still puzzled about how he had stumbled upon this underground world. Back in 1995, he had been running a computer company. He had always been at the top of his game, but a continued streak of bad luck had pushed his company to the brink of bankruptcy. Desperate and unsure of what to do, he knew he couldn't afford to keep hiring regular employees—he needed individuals with exceptional skills and talent. But he couldn't find any. In fact, he never would have until July 7, 1995.

That night, he was at a casino, squandering his last bit of cash on a game when someone made a striking comment about his strategy.

"What did you just say?" James asked the non-American man who sat with an air of composure, his face partially hidden from view.

"I said, you play for the long run. That's why you lose big. Games like these require a cutthroat strategy. Thinking big scale makes you lose. See, that guy will eat it all up."

And like a prophecy, the man's words came true. James lost every last bit of cash he had put into the game.

"How did you know?" James asked, eyes narrowing.

The man chuckled as he rose. "I didn't."

"What?"

"I didn't know. It's just… complicated. Sorry about the game. I'll see you around."

"Wait," James called after him, rushing to keep up. "Wait."

The man turned slightly but kept walking.

"Are you looking for… a job?" James cringed at how desperate he sounded.

"Do I look like I need one?"

"I'm sorry, it's just… a man with your abilities must be in high demand."

The man laughed. Just then, a car pulled over beside him. "Where are you headed?" he asked.

"Me? Wherever you're going," James replied.

"Hop in," the man grinned.

That one night introduced James to the leader of the extraction market. He was German, and his name was A. G. Griss. The man helped James reignite his company, showering him with countless favors. When James asked what Griss wanted in return, the man simply said he would know in due time.

And then the time came. James had gone over to Griss' mansion. Over the months, the two had become great acquaintances. James discovered that Griss possessed an extraordinary range of talents, and he couldn't help but envy the man.

"There's something I must discuss with you, James," Griss said one day as they sat outside his expansive mansion, watching the servants play golf.

James nodded, waiting patiently.

"You must envy my gifts... everything I do, my skills, my powers, everything..."

"That is true," James admitted.

"Imagine what it would be like to have a market where such powers are for sale... where you can purchase the ability to predict what will happen in six... seven years."

"Are you speaking of a talent market?"

"Something of that sort, yes."

"Well, it's quite a dream, but I think it would have a ghastly impact... honestly, I don't think our world is ready for such a market."

"Speak for yourself, James. The world is ready for a lot of things. We only fear what it would make us into."

James nodded nervously, unsure of the relevance of what the man was saying.

"What if I told you that such a market already exists? Would you believe me?"

"It's a hard sell, but again, considering your abilities, it's... not too impossible to imagine."

"There is, in fact, such a market... I created it."

James stared at the man, trying to maintain a straight face. "Wait, you're serious."

"I am..."

"It's impossible."

"It's not particularly legal, so you wouldn't hear about it..."

"You're really serious?" James stifled a grin.

"Follow me."

They walked to the man's study, facing a wall filled with books. Suddenly, Griss hit a switch, and a hidden door swung open. A staircase stretched infinitely downward, and they followed it into an underground facility teeming with darkness.

With the click of a switch, the place was flooded with light, revealing a host of humans in lab coats moving back and forth beyond a large window.

"What in God's name?" James muttered.

"Welcome," Griss said, "to the Hive."

The Hive, as Griss explained, was a research facility directly beneath his mansion. Their goal was simple: to identify, befriend, and extract gifts from extraordinarily talented individuals. The abilities were then sold to clients across the world. It was an unusual market, with a single talent sale grossing close to millions of dollars.

Griss showed him a chart displaying client bids on various talents. Several charts highlighted unextracted talents roaming the streets of America, with a few scattered beyond its borders.

James stared at the facility, wide-eyed, marveling at the impossibility of it all. In that moment, he knew he wanted to be part of this game. And before he could even voice his thoughts, Griss made the offer himself.

"I need your help, James."

James listened intently. This man was like a god in the flesh—the savior of his company.

"There's a man I've been tracking for decades. He possesses an extraordinary talent that two clients are bidding highly for. His gift is worth billions."

"How can I help?"

"It's simple how it works. I need you to hire him and have him work with you for two years."

"Two years is a long shot. Can't you just kidnap him or something?"

"No. How it works is rather complicated. To extract a person's ability, they need to come into contact with our process and machine for an extended period."

"And can't we just make a deal with these guys and have them sell it over?"

"It doesn't work that way… they do not practice or even know their strengths."

James pondered the rhetoric and nodded. He understood what his friend was driving at.

"Besides, it comes with repercussions," Griss said as they strode forward, stopping in front of a fridge-sized container with a woman's face inside it.

"She was a programmer. The best in the world. Picked her up in Asia. She was the first extraction."

"What… what happened to her?" James asked, his eyes glued to the pretty lady.

Griss sighed, walking away. "We couldn't save her—she died after she came out of the extraction machine. Since then, we've improvised. We have some new scientists on our team."

* * *

James kept staring at the chart highlighting the worth of Chandra's ability. He had been wrong about its value. It wasn't double her father's—it was triple. That was why they had commenced extraction procedures quickly.

The system worked simply: the statistics highlighted specific talents, providing insights into their real-life applications. Some talents were more in demand than others, while some were rare. Few ever crossed both margins. Chandra's ability was in high demand, making it unusually pricey. Since they had uploaded a trailer showcasing her talent, they had received about four hundred thousand bids for the ability to get into a picture gift.

* * *

James grinned to himself. Indeed, Griss was smart. He had given James the file of a certain man his sources had identified—Anurag Roy. Anurag was an Out-of-Body practitioner who had learned from leading practitioners in Tarapith, a holy city in India.

Over the following week, Griss walked him through ways to ensure Anurag would listen. He provided strategies and even suggested securing US-funded scholarships for Anurag's children. The unsuspecting Indian had felt indebted to James, unaware that he was merely a profitable investment. According to Griss, people with such talents had a tendency to pass them on to their offspring.

For as long as Anurag had been part of the business, James had kept a close eye on the entire Roy family—especially their children.

James stared at the stacks of data and smiled, his gaze shifting to the photo of the founder of Extraction Sales.

* * *

Priya sat in bed, watching her fiancé snore. Karan hadn't slept this soundly in a long time. When she was sure he was fast asleep, she slipped out through the main door and hurried to a section of the garage he rarely visited.

Taking out her phone, she dialed a number. Two rings in, the call clicked.

"Any luck?"

"Nothing yet."

"Okay. Try not to lose him..."

"And the family?"

"We can't talk about them now. Just stay low—you can't afford to blow your cover."

The line went dead. Priya wiped her eyes, sniffed, and headed back inside. But as she reached the bedroom, she froze.

Karan's bed was empty.

"Where were you?" Karan's voice came from a corner of the room.

"I... I heard voices outside. I went to check—"

"Voices? Where?" Karan hurried to the window.

"It was... it was nothing..."

"It can't be nothing."

"It's nothing, my love. Go to bed," Priya said, pressing a kiss to his cheek.

Karan sighed and sat on the bed. "I can't... I can't sleep."

"Why, my love?"

"Nightmares," he murmured, running a hand over his face. "I've been reaching out to people... waking them up."

"It'll be alright," Priya whispered, drawing close and wrapping her arms around him.

"Tell me about your nightmares" Priya said.

"It's... crazy. I keep seeing my dad... it's strange. It's like he's stuck somewhere, floating, and then suddenly, everything goes black. I can hear Mom's voice... she's scared. And then someone's trying to shoot us..."

"Shoot you?"

Karan nodded lightly. "There are gunshots. Someone was murdered, and then... that's it. I can't recall what else I saw..."

Priya shrugged, wrapping her arms around him. "Just a bad dream."

Karan hugged her. She was slightly surprised, but he had been like this since returning from police custody.

"I love you, Priya… I'm glad I met you… I love you…"

Priya smiled, unable to move her mouth, unsure how to respond to this unusual change in the man before her. Before, it had been easier to lie, but now, with his transformation, she wasn't sure she could keep up. This life, the lies—everything. How would she say it? When should she say it? Was it even possible? After all those trips to his family home, after everything...

She hadn't always been sure she had charmed him. She had tried hard and failed miserably. And yet, the fruit of all her labor was starting to show—a labor she had hoped would bear no fruit.

Karan had been a hard man. That was what had made everything seem easier. It was easy to pretend to a hard man.

But now, he was soft. Soft and meek. And he was professing his love to—

Priya buried her face in Karan's bare chest, her eyes growing moist. Karan was surprised to see her weep. He hated himself—for all the things he had done to her. All the fights, the complaints, everything. In the last few days, he had come to realize how much he needed someone. And Priya had always been there for him, yet he had ignored her.

He felt grateful. To hell with the world. To hell with the company. He had Priya. He had everything he needed.

Running his hand through her hair, he thought of the words he had just spoken. He had told her he loved her—and tears ran down her cheeks.

Chapter 17

January 1, 2020, Chicago

The 8:30 a.m. alarm woke Karan up. It felt harsher than the previous day. Raindrops poured from the sky as a pale sun took over the horizon.

Karan rose from the bed, his eyes drifting to Priya as sunlight touched the side of her face. He was tempted to reach out, to kiss her. But he couldn't. There was work to do, and his head throbbed from yet another dream—one where he had been abducted. Glancing at the clock, he hurried to the bathroom. He had a backlog of paperwork to catch up on after missing work the previous day.

Seconds later, he stepped out, towel-drying his neck as he made his way to the kitchen. By the time he was dressed, Priya was awake.

"Good Morning, Hon, and a Happy New Year. Sorry for a really bad New Years eve, this year, all on me. You are looking beautiful," Karan said, sliding a tray of tea next to her.

"M—morning," Priya mumbled, stretching. "Oh my, thanks—"

"No, thank you," Karan said, planting a kiss on her forehead before turning to knot his tie.

"You're heading to work on a holiday?" Priya asked, blowing on her tea.

"No. First, I need to visit someone."

"Is it a woman?" Priya grinned mischievously.

Karan turned to her, sitting by her while struggling with his tie, a smug grin on his lips. "Why would I want to go see a woman?"

"I don't know." Priya shrugged. "Let me help you with that."

Karan smiled as she helped him weave the tie. She brushed his shoulder when she was done.

"You look sharp, my love. Promise me you won't talk to any woman."

"What can I say? I'm a lucky man." Karan winked.

"Haha, tell me about it."

Karan put on his suit and ran a hand through his hair, glaring at the mirror. He turned to Priya, raising a brow.

"Fantastic," Priya said.

"I'll see you in a bit," Karan said, touching her lips before dashing out.

"Oh, and I'll be borrowing your car."

"And I was going to get an oil change done." Priya pouted.

"Not to worry, I'll drop by the car dealer—just today, I promise."

"Alright."

Karan waved as he left.

"Oh, wait!" Priya called back. "An email came in for you."

"It can wait."

"It looks urgent."

"When I'm back, sweetie," Karan called out as he disappeared into the broad daylight.

Seconds later, the sound of a car roared to life before drifting into the streets. Priya leaned against the glass window, watching Karan zoom out of their garage. When he was out of sight, she dashed back inside, shut the window and doors, and pulled out her laptop. It had been on the whole night. A video call was waiting for her. The instant she logged on, a face appeared on the screen.

"He just stepped out," she said.

"Have you been able to find it?"

"I've looked everywhere. If he has it, it's not here."

"Where did he go?"

"The office. He'll be visiting a car dealer later today."

The face on the other end relaxed. "We'll have to intercept him there."

Priya went silent.

"You must understand, it's the only way."

Priya opened her mouth to speak—and stopped.

"What, you don't want to see your family?"

"Of course, I do."

"Then stop fooling around."

"It's… it's just that… he's starting to…"

"Is he suspicious?"

"No, nothing of that sort… it's just… he's… different."

"Keep your eyes on the mission. There's a lot at stake here."

Priya nodded. "I'll do my best."

"You better."

* * *

Karan was stuck in traffic. He had been trying to call someone from the office, but no one was picking up. And then there were the bloody morons blaring their horns behind him. Finally, a call went through.

"I've been trying your line all day. Where the hell have you all been?"

"I'm sorry, sir, there's some—"

Honk honk!

"I can't hear you." Karan craned his neck outside, shooting an evil gaze at the jeep behind him. "You were saying…"

"The office—"

Honk honk honk!

Karan gritted his teeth, yelling at the guys behind him to stop. But...

Hoooooooooooooooooooooooonnnnnnnnnkkkkkkk!

By now, Karan's face was red. He jumped out of the car and stormed toward the jeep. He knocked on the window, about to speak when it rolled down—and a lady poked her head out, aiming a gun at him.

"Get in."

Karan was stuck in the jeep as it sped off.

"That's my fiancée's car!" he kept saying as they drove off the highway through an exit. He could still make out Priya's KIA at the spot where he had left it. Goodness, he never got to lock the windows!

"That's my fiancée's—"

"Not to worry, she'll get it back in one piece… can't say the same about you, though." The lady grinned, shooting him a stare.

Her face was unlike anything he had ever seen. There were two other men in the back, but their expressions were nothing compared to the lady's unusually monstrous glare. Her face was sharp and chiseled, and she smelled as if she had slept in a rose garden.

"Who are you… what do you want?"

The woman behind the wheel nodded to the men in the back, and they threw a dark fabric over Karan's face, plunging his world into total darkness.

"Karan, as much as I regret to say this, the lives of the people you love may gravely depend on your cooperation."

Back on the highway, where the KIA was parked, a man jumped out of a different car that had been stationed not too far away. He had seen them abduct Karan and was speaking rapidly into a radio.

* * *

Karan skidded forward as the vehicle came to a halt, smashing his face against the hard back of the driver's seat. As he tried to regain balance, his hearing sharpened. They were in a large, empty space—he could tell from the echoes as the car pulled in.

He heard doors click open before two pairs of arms yanked him out of the car. He squinted hard, trying to see through the fabric over his head, but it was futile. Whatever they had put on him was designed to blind him, preventing him from seeing where he was or how he got there.

Footsteps echoed as they walked through the silent space, each step amplifying the surroundings. They climbed some brief stairs and soon entered an elevator. Karan could tell from the soft chime each time they passed a floor.

"Seat him there," the woman's rough voice commanded.

Karan felt a chair beneath him as he was forced down. The covering was pulled off, and the cool air from an air conditioner brushed against his damp face. His heart pounded furiously as he looked around.

Were they going to kill him? Were Abhi and Chandra in the same facility?

Good god… was this the end for him?

Only then did Karan remember he had dreamt of this exact occurrence just that morning. It was absurd. Was he seeing visions again? He gazed at the two men standing before him, their hands folded over their belts, their eyes fixed on him. Karan noticed they hadn't tied him up. These men didn't look friendly, yet this didn't feel like a typical kidnapping.

His eyes wandered past them, taking in the office they were in. Framed photos lined the walls. A door creaked open, and the woman walked in—her face just as mean as before. Behind her, a man followed.

The man approached Karan directly, his sweat-drenched sleeves rolled up.

"Hello, Mr. Roy. I must apologize for the rough treatment. We're not always this direct," he said.

"Who... who are you?" Karan asked.

"I am Anthony Stein, deputy director of our little service outfit." He gestured toward the others. "I believe you've met Gloria, Ralph, and Socks. We call ourselves Tony's, and we like to keep our country clean. We're in the crime-cleaning business."

Karan stared at Stein quizzically. "Tony's?"

"That's right. You're here because... we need your help."

"My help? Now would be a bad time, Mr. Stein. I have a lot to do—"

"Where?"

"At the office," Karan said confidently.

"You mean this office?"

Stein pulled out a remote and pressed a button. A screen lit up, showing live footage of Karan's office building. A crowd had gathered outside. Karan leaned in. Those weren't just passersby—they were his employees. They stood there as law enforcement agents evacuated the premises. A yellow tape stretched across the entrance, reading "Closed by court order."

"Is this the office you were trying to get to, Mr. Roy? Because it doesn't look like they'll be needing you anytime soon."

Karan couldn't take his eyes off the screen. He watched his workers, clueless and stranded, as their only means of livelihood was put on indefinite hold.

"What..." Karan managed to say. "What do you want?"

Stein clicked the remote, and the footage of the building vanished. It was replaced by the image of a man—one Karan still remembered all too well.

"I believe you know this man, Mr. Roy," Stein said, rolling up the sleeve of his slumped-down shirt.

"What does this have to do with anything?"

"Oh, a lot."

"Some twenty years ago," Gloria stepped forward, "this man, Anurag Roy, disappeared after a trip to Chicago. He was last seen entering a taxi, after which he seemingly vanished. No trace of the taxi, no ransom demands—nothing. All police records have been wiped. He just vanished."

"We believe you already know this, Mr. Karan," Stein said.

Karan took a deep breath, his gaze fixed on the eyes staring back at him from the screen.

"Our records show," Gloria continued, "that you came in contact with a certain Ross Loffers, requesting he reopen the investigation—"

"It… it wasn't a request."

"Could you elaborate, please?" Stein said calmly from where he was seated.

"The thing is… I," Karan exhaled with some difficulty, "I was talking to Ross about it, and… and he thought it was weird that the previous investigators had given up on the case without further probes."

"And this Ross, where is he now?"

Karan broke eye contact with Stein, licking his lips as the terrible memory of Ross's body resurfaced.

"Dead," Karan said.

"No." Stein rose, pointing at the screen. "Murdered, Mr. Roy. He was murdered… under the strict instruction of the same man he was trying to uncover…"

"What… what are you saying? That my father had him killed?"

"No," Gloria said, tapping the remote so that a new photo appeared on the screen. The image showed a gathering at a table.

At the bar, a man was sipping a glass of wine. Karan sat up the moment he saw the man's face.

"This... this is impossible... When was this recorded? When?" Karan demanded, his eyes fixed on the familiar face.

"January the sixth," Stein said.

Karan's jaw fell open.

"Mr. Karan, we believe your father," Gloria said, "...is alive."

Karan stared wide-eyed at Gloria and Stein, trying to process their words.

"We believe Mr. Anurag Roy is running a dirty operation... and we are tasked with nabbing him."

"Nab him?" Karan cut in, noticing how the two took turns speaking like a rehearsed act.

"Yes, Mr. Karan. Was your father not a specialist in the human mind?"

"I remember little about my father," Karan lied. Of course, he remembered a lot. Sumati had told them enough stories to last a lifetime. Even then, Karan recalled how his father often went out with Abhi on matters that never interested him. Karan had no passion for deep studies of the human mind, but he knew his dad, brother, and sister were deeply involved in it. Somehow, Karan had always been closer to his mother. These questions were meant for Abhi, not him.

"I remember little about my father, so I have little insight into what you're hinting at."

"Alright. Gloria, tell him."

"We believe your father," Gloria continued, "...had abilities. Unusual abilities that extended beyond what could be measured through scientific means. Before his disappearance, he had been working on a prototype—a computer program. Here's his proposal. The program was designed to achieve impossible feats, like mind-reading, by simply analyzing facial and body movements, breaking them into micro-gestures, and drawing solid conclusions from hormones, blood flow, heartbeat, and other bodily functions."

Karan stared wide-eyed. "It's... it's impossible. My dad was smart, but he wasn't some human engineer," he shot back, boiling with cold rage. These accusations were becoming preposterous. He was already drowning in stress—the office shutdown, Ross' death, Abhi, Chandra, and Sumati going missing. Now, he was being told his father was alive and, even worse, trying to destroy the world. And with what? A computer program?

Karan tried to catch his breath. After all these years, his old man was really alive, still breathing somewhere on this planet, sipping a glass of wine while his family had been in shambles over his disappearance.

"Are you into science fiction, Karan?" Stein asked.

Karan took a breath, lines stretching across his forehead as he tried to recall something.

"It's a hybrid of profound futurist ideas and literature. The best of them encompass dystopian worlds, top-notch technology, etc. Most of it is inspired by human biology and AI anthropology. We believe your father was working on a dystopian program before his disappearance. In fact, we think he staged his disappearance to continue the project"

"You think? And all of this is based on assumptions?" Karan said.

"We have proof to back this claim. He may also be involved in Borda's death."

"There you go again," Karan thought to himself. First, it was Abhi who was involved with Borda—now it was their father.

"And you will, except there's not enough time. We have a few questions for you."

"I'm not saying jack sh** until I know who you guys are and see some proof..."

"Please! Besides, how do you think your fiancée would react if we were to deliver her car with its front part crushed?"

Karan swallowed hard and said gently, "She's my fiancée."

"A better reason to cooperate, don't you think? What better way to keep a woman than to keep her car safe?"

Karan nodded quickly. "W…what do you wish to know?"

Stein pulled his chair closer to Karan. "Karan, is there a chance you've acquired certain traits from your father…?"

"I don't understand…"

"I mean characteristics—things you normally wouldn't be able to do, but because Mr. Anurag Roy is your father, you can."

"I beg your pardon." Karan's eyes flared.

"What Mr. Stein is saying," Gloria stepped in, "is—do you have special abilities?"

Karan swallowed, his eyes shifting between the two. For a moment, he thought they were about to pounce on him. He avoided making direct eye contact with Gloria as he spoke.

"No."

"No, as in?" Stein asked.

"I don't have abilities."

"And your siblings? Abhi, Chandra—do they have any?" Stein leaned back.

"No, none that I'm aware of."

Stein nodded and walked off.

"Ehm, one last thing… Karan, my apologies, we'll soon be done with you. Are you in contact with Abhi and Chandra?"

"Emm… well, Abhi was with me at the site where we found Ross'… body…"

"And when was that?"

"About two days ago…" Karan said, confident he'd be out of here soon.

"Show him," Stein said to Gloria.

Gloria tapped the remote, and the screen flickered to life, showing a masked man pushing a large trolley with a tall carton box, about to load it into a van.

"This is your sister's neighborhood, is that correct, Mr. Karan?"

Karan's lips parted as he spoke. "Y…yes… what's going on?"

"Karan, we believe your sister may have been abducted."

Chapter 18

December 31, 2019, Somewhere

Abhi woke with a start, a bitter taste lingering at the back of his tongue. Where was he? His head felt foggy and heavy, and for a moment, he held it between his arms, fearing it would fall off his shoulders at any moment. As he touched his head, he felt something on his face—a pipe of some sort.

He rushed to a mirror on the wall, and his heart clenched. He gazed at the reflection of the object on his head. It wasn't really a pipe—it was more of a hose. It was connected to his head, extending into the ceiling. Panicking, he tried to force it off.

"I wouldn't do that if I were you."

The corners of the room echoed with the voice. It seemed like an AI generated voice—one of those digital types that warped a person's tone into something sinister and machine-like.

Abhi looked around for the first time. The room was small and airtight, its walls made of steel except for one side, which held a large mirror. He scanned his surroundings. There was no one there.

On the other side of the reflective glass, a team of scientists watched him, their many eyes alternating between their monitors and the man in the glass. But Abhi could not see them.

"We're here. Look up," the voice came again, and Abhi glared at the ceiling. It was well sealed except for a few depressions on its surface, where a net-like metal fabric covered them.

Speakers, Abhi thought. They were speakers.

He tried to force the hose off his head again but found himself growing more exhausted with each attempt.

"Relax. We're here with you."

"What have you done to me?" Abhi asked, staggering as he kept his eyes on the speaker in the ceiling.

"You've been under our watch for the past few hours..."

"F...few hours? It's...felt like months..."

"It's only been a few hours, I assure you."

"What day is it?"

* * *

There was some hesitation on Dr. X's part. She glanced at James, who leaned toward the little mic.

"It's been one day," James said.

Dr. X faltered at his words. The man in the box could sense something wasn't right.

"What have you done to m...me...?"

"We assure you, there's—"

"Get me out of here!" His voice cut Dr. X off.

"We will—"

"Get me out of here, right now! Now—"

The man broke into a coughing fit. He staggered forward, gasping. At that moment, James had already sent in a team. The steel doors opened, and multiple men in face masks hurried in. They lifted him and carried him to a different lab.

"What was that about?" James asked as they left the room and headed into his office.

"It's like we said. He rejects it. Anurag may have invented one, but there's no telling how he did it. It's... complex."

"Alright... the girl. What about the girl?"

"Procedures for extraction will commence shortly," Dr. X said.

"Alright."

Just then, the door swung open, and a man in a white uniform walked in.

"Sir," the man said, hurrying to his side. Before whispering in James' ear. James' face lit up. He swung towards Dr. X.

"Thanks, Dr. X. That will be all." James said. Dr. X glanced at James before leaving the room. James turned to the man.

"Now, what in the world did you just say?"

* * *

Dr. X hurried back to the lab. She looked around, making sure no one was there before inserting a USB into the system. She was uploading a different habit program—one far from what they were trying to replicate. She had her reasons. She had ensured that the man they had just put to sleep would never accept the program. Now, she needed a way to communicate with him—to help him escape.

Dr. X adjusted her glasses, pondering the consequences of being caught. Oh, the things James would do to her. She had known James for a long time. She had met Anurag around the same time.

A sharp pain stabbed at her heart. She had betrayed Anurag. She recalled how it had all happened.

She had been the bait they set for him. For weeks, the two had spent time together. She had pretended to be a specialist in human relations. Every time they met, it was in the same hotel room. He had told her he'd gained unusual access to the hotel's exquisite suite through work, and she had nodded sheepishly, holding back the truth. She couldn't tell him.

How could she tell him that the notorious benefactor who granted him exclusive access to the hotel and all the quiet luxuries of Chicago life was someone she knew too well?

How could she tell him that in the same room where he slept every night, a device was preparing him neurologically for extraction?

How could she tell him she had known all along?

How could she?

She shut her eyes as the memory of their last meeting unfolded like a movie. It had been a beautiful night. A cab wove through the busy Chicago streets, coming to a halt outside a towering structure that stretched endlessly into the night sky. She stepped out of the car, her black dress hugging her frame. October was only hours away, and it felt like the perfect evening to spend with a friend.

She made her way up the stairs and through the revolving glass doors of the hotel, her heels clacking against the oyster-white tiles of the reception floor.

"Good evening," she said to the man at the front desk.

"A wonderful evening to you, ma'am. How can I assist?"

"I'm meeting someone here." She mentioned her host's name.

"One moment, please," the receptionist said, running a gloved hand down a list. He grabbed the phone on the desk and made a call. Seconds later, he nodded.

"Follow me, please," he said. "He's been expecting you."

He guided her to the elevator while another man took over at the front desk. She took a deep breath as the elevator began to climb, its bells chiming with each passing floor. Finally, at the hundredth floor, the doors hissed open, revealing the open exterior of the hotel's top floor.

"He's out there," he said, gesturing toward a man standing in the distance with his back turned to them.

Jenny nodded at the receptionist just as the elevator doors closed. She trudged toward the man, her knees trembling as she fully grasped the frightening reality—she was at the edge of a rooftop.

Goodness, she could fall at any moment. But it was just her nerves reacting to something she had always fantasized about—dining at an exquisite hotel, out in the open, under the dark Chicago sky. She just never imagined *this* man would be the one to treat her to it, let alone on a supposedly *platonic* date.

The man turned around, a bone-deep smile spreading across his face like a virus. The wind tousled his hair, and with the lights of the dark city behind him, he looked as if he were floating in deep space.

"Welcome," he said, pulling out a chair for her near the edge of the roof, where a short wall lined the perimeter.

"This is crazy," she said, managing an awkward laugh.

"I thought you were crazier." He winked, and they shared a laugh.

A breeze of silence settled between them, their gazes locked long enough to make them break into another fit of laughter. It was things like this she liked about him—his ability to be both manly and childish at the same time. She wanted to jump into his lap and squeeze him in a hug.

For God's sake, be civil.

After another long pause, he spoke.

"Do you like the view?"

"God, yes... it's... dangerously fascinating." She giggled, her hands trembling on the table.

He reached forward, taking them in his. Then he leaned in.

"Dangerously fascinating, huh? Sounds like someone I know."

"Awwwh." She purred.

"Don't get too impressed—I wasn't talking about you." He chuckled, withdrawing his hand playfully.

Her smile widened, her cheeks starting to ache from laughing too hard. He tried to recover from his own laughter, spilling a bit of wine as he refilled her glass.

"Thank you," she said, gracefully sipping from the glass, her gaze drawn to the vast, light-flooded city stretching around them. She was genuinely impressed that he had done this for her.

"You look..." he said, a glint of light in his eyes, "you... look ravishing."

He meant it. She could've sworn he meant it. She hid her cheeks as they flushed.

"Of course, I am. I mean, it's me after all." She tossed her hair with a playful smirk.

He grinned, sipping his glass. They went on, talking about the weather, the city, work, Shakespeare, food. They talked about nothing and everything. It was an ordinary time out—nothing serious.

Moments later, they were strolling through a mini aquatic museum, home to some of the rarest sea creatures. They stopped at a section showcasing the oldest kissing seahorses.

"Hey, break it off," she giggled, clapping her hands to get their attention.

"Why bother them? Why can't we just appreciate two lovers romancing in the peace of this night?"

She threw her head back, sniggering. "Haha, don't even go there."

He turned to her, and for a moment, her heart stopped beating.

"I swear... it's easy," he said, a glint sparkling in his eyes, their faces barely inches apart.

She swallowed, staring into those eyes, angels singing in her stomach. They were close. Dangerously close.

They kissed. And though she went home upset the next morning, she would come to cherish the memory.

Dr. X recovered from the short trip to twenty-plus years ago. The funny thing was, he himself had perfected the program they had used on him.

Dr. X leaned forward, her eyes on the progress bar. The file transfer was at 76%.

"Doctor." The door swung open, ushering in her assistant.

"Hey!" Dr. X was startled, quickly blocking the screen. "Hey, Leisha… w-what are you… shouldn't you be home?"

"Yeah, sorry, I thought I'd drop in on you… forgot my purse." Leisha, her assistant held up her purse, trying to sneak a peek at the screen. "I see you're still working on the program?"

"Um… yes." Dr. X inhaled before stepping away from the screen. It was blank.

"Wait, that's a blank screen."

She winked. "Staring at a black blank screen has a way of… I don't know, helping me calm down."

"Weirded out."

"That's why it works. Hey, did you get dinner?"

"I'm game. On me this time," Leisha said.

Leisha left to save a table for the two.

* * *

January 1, 2020, Chicago

Karan drove back to his apartment. He remained behind the wheel, the sound of chirping crickets and frogs in the distance. It was dark in the car; he hadn't turned the lights on. He rubbed his face, pondering everything Stein and Gloria had said. Was it all true? Was his father alive? And Abhi and Chandra…

His heartbeat skipped at the thought.

Just then, he saw the window of his house light up, and the blinds were pulled to the side. Priya's face emerged, waiting for him to come in. Karan got out of the car.

"Is everything okay?" Priya asked as she trudged in.

He grunted, nodding as he sat on the couch.

"You look pale. Are you alright?"

"Water," Karan said. "I need water."

Priya came back with a bottle. She was filling a glass when he shook his head, grabbed it, and took a deep, long gulp. The bottle was empty by the time it fell to the floor. Only then did Karan realize just how thirsty he was.

"It... was a great day..." he smiled, turning to her. "Hectic, but great."

He kissed her face and rose, heading to their room.

"Dinner is ready."

"Alright, my love, give me a moment to change and shower..."

An hour went by, but Karan did not come to the table. Priya went to check on him—the bathroom door was open, and the floor was dry. He hadn't even been there.

She hurried to their bedroom... and sighed.

Lying on the bed, still in his suit and tie, Karan was snoring like a baby.

"Truly a great day," Priya whispered.

Chapter 19

January 1, 2020, Chicago

The lights flickered on, revealing a massive glass enclosure at the center of the room. Wires snaked from its base into a power receptor. Abhi noticed fiber cables connected to his head.

Monitors lined the walls, and the ceiling pulsed with blue lights. Dr. X stood before the enclosure, tapping a few keys on a display, while Leisha and James observed from a distance.

"Is he logged in yet?" James asked. "Happy New Year, X. Were you here all night?"

"One moment," Dr. X replied, watching the ignition bar fill. "He'll be logged in... now."

A deep hum echoed from the enclosure as streaks of color and light surged through the fiber cables linked to Abhi's brain. The virtual display came to life—at that moment, Abhi started screaming.

Abhi felt sucked into a black hole. In the distant nothingness, there was a dot—a tiny speck of light. Slowly, the speck emerged into a spiral. This green spiral circled endlessly against the backdrop of infinite void. Right there, he felt his muscles relax. The spiral went on forever, spinning and spinning. And spinning—an endless loop, fascinating to watch, tampering with deep things in the core of his psyche. But of course, he didn't know that.

Soon, the spiral spread everywhere, in all directions. The dark void began to shrink like paint peeling off a wall, colors bleeding into space, morphing into something that had air, light—life.

Structures emerged from the shadows of what had been a mere speck of light. Plants sprang from the void, a blank sky creeping through the firmament as tiny water droplets raged down in a downpour. It was raining. Abhi looked around in awe. He knew this place. All around him were plants and flowers—words couldn't begin to encompass them. He was in a garden. He knew this garden.

Abhi saw his young neighbors playing amid the bits of rain, water droplets falling and sizzling into specks of green pixels. Unknowingly, he had teleported to his old house.

Where is Chandra? he asked himself.

A blinding green light engulfed the area, threatening to fry his eyeballs.

Darkness.

Silence.

Click clack, click clack, click clack…

He was back in his confinement room, with a window to the lawn outside. It was dark, eternally dark, and he could hear footsteps approaching. Faint but consistent. Slowly, bits of light crept in from the window. Someone was walking there.

A man.

As he drew closer, Abhi froze. Anurag Roy was staring right at him.

* * *

"We're making headway!" Leisha called back from the monitor.

Dr. X swallowed hard. She saw the readings and knew he was ready for extraction. Lowering his stress level had been crucial—

extraction was complicated, and withdrawing his abilities would be impossible if his subconscious remained on guard.

"Good work, Doctor," James said.

Dr. X blinked at him, her glare softening. Her lips almost curled into a smile before she turned abruptly and hurried through the doors.

"She must be very excited," Leisha said, watching her go.

Leisha was wrong.

* * *

Dr. X's mind was a scrambled puzzle as she raced to the bathroom, nearly tripping. She turned the taps on, splashing cold water on her face as her hands trembled.

What if Abhi dies?

It was her fault. All of it.

She wiped her face clean, staring into the mirror. A stranger stared back—a woman cloaked in the authority of a lead scientist, supposedly in charge of manipulating the human subconscious. A gnawing emptiness was tearing her apart.

Frantically, she dug through her purse, searching for her meds. Her fingers closed around the red container, and she popped the lid open.

Empty.

Her breath hitched. She bolted from the bathroom, still shaking.

* * *

All that fuss earlier had been a cry of joy, Leisha thought. Dr. X seemed calm now, wearing her usual smile.

Yet, to Leisha, her expression felt cold. She smiled back anyway, sipping her trophy tea. It was a grand milestone they had just accomplished—finally, the subject was ready for extraction.

She observed the rows of data scrolling across the screen and wondered how the subject himself was feeling. All they had were raw numbers. Unless you were a data scientist, you'd have no clue what each code meant. To Leisha, the lines appeared abstract. Technically speaking, the team couldn't actually see his emotions—unless some mad psychic genius invented a machine capable of displaying complex, hidden desires unknown even to the subject himself.

What they could do, however, was monitor brain impulses. Certain regions of the brain aligned with specific emotional responses—deep affection, empathy, indignation, regret, and more.

Through Dr. X's brilliance, they had managed to alter the subject's predisposition toward fear and indignation, shifting it into deep empathy. The perfect, relaxed state for extraction.

And Dr. X had figured it all out.

* * *

James got a call.

"What's so good?"

"You have to see this right away. I'm sending you a video."

James opened it on his PC, his jaw dropping.

"When was this?"

"His last trip to Delhi."

James wiped his eyes and played the video again. And again. And again.

"My god, this is unbelievable," he murmured, his gaze locked on the screen.

Finally, he grinned and leaned toward the phone receiver.

"How much do you think this would go for?"

* * *

January 2, 2020, Chicago

The clock read five in the morning.

Karan jumped out of bed, racing to the kitchen as hunger gnawed at him. Luckily, Priya had packed the leftovers he hadn't eaten, leaving them in the refrigerator. He pulled out the salad and salmon steak, tossing the steak into the microwave while he munched on the cold, crispy salad.

He was biting down greedily when he looked up and saw Priya standing in the doorway, wrapped in her PJs, rubbing her eyes. She watched him devour his meal like a starving rodent.

"Happy New Year! We were supposed to go downtown," she said.

"Hey… that was a big miss," he replied between mouthfuls.

"You vanished."

Karan spread sauce between two slices of bread, nodding. "Yeah, sorry about last night. I was really exhausted."

"It's okay, baby, with everything going on. You must be starving now."

"You have no idea," Karan said, bobbing his head.

"I couldn't help but notice—you never visited the car dealer like you said you would…"

Karan hesitated, his mouth slightly open. "Will… will do… um, later. Got caught up on…"

"It's nothing, really. It's just that I have to leave early today. I've got an interview at nine, and I'm hoping the car doesn't break down."

"Not to worry," Karan said, slurping from a mug of tea. "You'll be fine."

"Hope so."

"Trust me, Priya. You've managed to put up with my stubbornness—what could be worse than that?" Karan chuckled.

Priya smiled, retreating into the room.

"Hey," she called out midway, "don't forget—you have a lot of emails to check."

"Will do, thanks," Karan replied, his mouth still full. He was still hungry.

After his quick breakfast, he sipped the old wine he had stored in his cellar since the inception of his company—a welcome 2020 drink. Ironic, he thought, that he was finally indulging in this vintage luxury just as he was on the verge of losing the company. Karan had a dark sense of humor. He grinned as he booted up his computer.

When he logged into his email, a flood of messages awaited him—2,989, to be exact. No wonder Priya had reminded him. He had borrowed her PC in the past, so she could always tell when his inbox was overloaded.

Karan scanned through the thousands of unread messages, wondering where to start. One was from the court. A few from his lawyers. Another from Legacy Inc., a client. Several from vendors.

But one email caught his eye.

Ignoring the pressing messages from familiar corporate names, Karan clicked on it the moment he saw the sender.

It was from Ross Loffers.

* * *

Stein was poring over video footage when Gloria walked in.

"We have a call," she said, handing him the phone.

"Who?"

"Him."

Stein pressed the phone to his ear. "Isn't it a bit early for a call, Mr. Roy?"

"I'm in."

Stein shifted in his seat. "I'm afraid I don't understand, Mr. Roy."

"Mr. Stein," the voice crackled through the speaker, "I'm in. I want to help."

The corner of Stein's lips curled upward as he stole a glance at Gloria. She was staring back at him, barely containing her excitement.

"This is a wise move, Mr. Roy. You won't regret it."

"I hope not."

"Please remain where you are. We'll send a team to collect you—"

"That won't be necessary."

Stein's eyebrows lifted. "And why's that?"

"Mr. Stein," Roy's voice rasped, "I'm outside your facility. Happy New Year!"

Chapter 20

January 2, 2020, Chicago

The extraction procedure for Chandra was set to begin, but Dr. X was nowhere to be found. The other scientists had searched for her, trying various ways to reach her, but she was unreachable.

"When was she last seen?" James asked the head of security as they reviewed the facility's surveillance footage.

"Earlier this morning. She was with one of the staff on level six, logging a complaint—something about a failure in the girl's pod."

"Pod failure? Run diagnostics."

"We did… it looks fine."

James' scowl deepened. "Why wasn't I informed? Where is she now?"

"No idea. Could be in the fields, the forest… can't say."

"Send a search team. She knows too much—we can't lose her. And if she's pulling a stunt on us… God help her." James motioned toward the door, then turned to Leisha.

"You. My office."

Leisha sat, hands on her knees, waiting.

James stared at her. "Tell me…"

She hesitated, waiting for more.

"Tell you what?"

"What you know… tell me what you know."

Leisha hesitated. "About Dr. X?"

James nodded.

"I... I'm shocked—"

"Bullshit!" James snapped, leaning forward. "You know something. I can tell."

"I... I don't understand—"

"Don't play dumb, Leisha."

She sighed, removing her glasses. "All I know is that the other day, I walked into the lab. She was... working on the copy."

"Dr. X..."

"Yes. She was up to something. I didn't know what, but it seemed important."

"What did you see?"

"She had a USB plugged in. I thought she was rewriting the program."

"You thought."

"Affirmative, sir."

"And you can confirm this, one hundred percent?"

"Not exactly, but... Dr. X and I are close. She wouldn't hide anything from me."

James studied her. "Is that so? Leisha, do you know how many antidepressants she's taken in the last few days?"

Leisha blinked. "She uses those?"

"Yes. So, it's surprising that someone with an 'effective relaxation technique' is consuming antidepressants in large doses. Don't be gullible, Leisha."

"I have no idea what you're alluding to," Leisha said firmly, her voice cold, veins tensed. "But Dr. X has nothing to hide from me. If anything, the medication proves she's struggling and needs support."

Her heart pounded. She was never the type to lose her cool. But this was Dr. X they were talking about. How could he even suggest such a thing? She stared at her boss, fearing she had vexed him.

"Are you sure it was really a blank screen you saw, Leisha?"

Her jaw tightened. The implication that Dr. X would sabotage their work was infuriating.

"I'm certain I saw a black screen. It could've been anything. But I'm sure it's nothing to worry about. I may be wrong, but—"

"Send in the chemists."

Her eyes widened.

"Why?"

"Have them examine the virtual copy—verify there's no anomaly. And they're to compare it with the original."

Leisha sat there, turning his words over in her mind.

"Off you go," James dismissed.

"B-but…I'm not authorized to access that level."

"You are now. Until we find Dr. X, you're in charge of the scientists."

Leisha's face went pale. Had she just been given a field promotion? She pushed herself up, her legs stiff.

"I…I won't let you—"

"Just go."

* * *

Leisha suppressed a grin as she glared at the team of workers now under her lead. All of them, men and women of top prowess. And they would do exactly as she said.

"Dr. Leisha, take a look at this."

Dr. Leisha, is it?

She strolled over, stifling a wilder grin at the thought. She looked over the man's shoulder at the transparent display.

"What do we have?" she said, keeping her tone composed and boss-like.

"Something's off…the copy has been altered." He pointed at the screen.

Leisha followed the patterns. It was true. It wasn't the same as before.

"The authenticity," he said, "has dropped—seventy percent."

"How's that possible?" Leisha asked.

He shrugged, chewing on the butt of a pen.

"Compare it with the original one we lifted from Mr. A's brain scan," she said.

"That's the problem."

Leisha frowned. "What are you saying?"

The man hesitated. "Dr. Leisha, the original copy… it's missing."

* * *

January 2, 2020, Tony's HQ in Chicago

Karan tapped his hand on the armrest, two pairs of eyes glaring back at him. These eyes belonged to Deputy Director Stein and his maverick associate, Gloria. He had told them everything. They wouldn't stop glaring, their faces as shocked as when he showed up at the facility unannounced. Seconds later, Stein and Gloria left the room to debate in a secured space. Karan didn't mind. An hour had already passed since he arrived.

The two had been somewhat taken aback when he expressed his commitment to helping them unveil the mystery surrounding his father's disappearance. It was only natural. Following his last visit, they had kept him under a black veil when they returned him to Priya's KIA, the same one he had abandoned during his subtle road kidnap. But that was the least shocking thing.

Karan had dreamt the path—and other things he kept to himself.

Goosebumps rose on his skin as he recalled lines from Ross' email. His investigator friend had cracked the case on his own, tailing the cab driver who had picked up Anurag Roy back in 1999. The email mentioned something that would never have popped up on any radar had Ross not carefully observed the hidden tracks in the case. More important than the taxi driver, Ross had written, was a briefcase filled with counterfeit diamonds.

He had retrieved these diamonds from the apartment of the now-murdered taxi driver, whose deranged lifestyle had failed to attract deep investigative scrutiny. Ross had detailed how he found the counterfeit diamonds and their connection to the case. Karan shook his head when he learned about the counterfeit bribe Mr. Owen had received to take his father to an undisclosed location. The diamonds had been stored in a suitcase.

What made it even more interesting was the exclusive logo belonging to a luxury company.

And the best part?

Ross had identified the company.

It was Legacy Inc.

Karan had told all this to Gloria and Stein, adding that he had received an email from the same client that morning. Legacy Inc. was one of Karan's best clients. And now, they were requesting a meeting. It was at this point in the conversation that the two had sat there, stunned for what felt like hours before excusing themselves to hold a quick meeting in another room.

Karan was filled with awe and respect for Ross' work. In the latter part of the email, Ross had explained that he was being tailed. He feared for his life and had prepared the email in advance in case things ended badly for him. Karan had left this bit out during his explanation to Stein and Gloria.

The door creaked open, and Stein strolled in, the door closing shut behind him as he threw himself into the chair opposite Karan. He toyed with a miniature hawk he had picked up from the table, his legs propped on the desk as he eyed Karan with those calm flames he had for eyes.

"We accept your offer to assist our cause, Mr. Roy. The intel you have provided is really… essential to our cause. We are grateful."

"Mr. Stein, you should know, I'm not doing this without requests… I have demands."

"Demands? What do you think this is, a charity?"

Karan leaned back, picking at his nails as he let Stein blow off steam. "Ahhh, and what if we refuse your request?"

Karan smirked, leaning further back. "I'll take this story to law enforcement and won't seek your help anymore."

"And you think they'll believe you?" Stein scoffed.

"It's a wild card, but what do I have to lose? The call is, after all, anonymous."

Karan watched Stein grin awkwardly, fumbling with the miniature hawk. For a moment, he thought he saw him hesitate.

"Damn it!" Stein finally said, slamming the hawk onto his desk. "Okay, name your price, Karan."

"You know what I want, Mr. Stein."

Stein understood because he shook his head. "It's impossible. I can't do that."

"Yes, you can."

"Even if I tried, I can't guarantee it. It's a waste already, exploiting that loop—"

"Mr. Stein," Karan said, pointing at the miniature hawk in Stein's hands. "I did some research this morning and found that you have a lot of friends in high places."

Stein swallowed at that, the calm fire in his eyes now a raging furnace.

"You know people who can help me," Karan said, veins bulging from his neck. "Really powerful people."

Stein nodded carefully, slowly, then gave a light clap. "Who do you want, Karan? I'll have to speak to my superiors on this, but I tell you—no guarantees. My fingers are crossed."

Karan nodded as he rose. "I'll be expecting orders, Stein."

"Orders, you will get."

Karan turned to leave.

"Err, Karan..." Stein called, strolling towards him.

"Yes?"

Stein held the door and asked 'politely'.

"How on earth did you find us?"

Chapter 21

December 31, 2019, South Chicago

At a distant block not far from a bridge overlooking a lake, a jeep swerved left, snaking through a neighborhood. This was the heart of the suburbs, where bodies of junkies littered the streets.

Two women dressed in matching black stepped out of the jeep, moving past a thousand vacant eyes withering from excessive drug use. They reached a metal door and knocked in an absurd pattern. A metal slab swung open, revealing a set of wrinkled eyes glaring through the rectangular hole. Seconds later, the door creaked open, and the two marched in.

The place reeked of tobacco. Pushing forward, they walked through a curtain made of beads. At the far end stood a wall with peeling paint. A beggar sat with his back against it, chewing on a tobacco stick. He grinned at the two, revealing a good number of missing incisors.

He rose as they approached, leaning on two crutches to support his bad leg.

"Ya'll gotta go in slow. He don't want no disturbance—he's got guests," he said, the tobacco still stuck between his teeth.

With that, he stamped his palm against a metal casing on the wall. A loud hum filled the room as the paint on the wall paled, revealing a steel door that swung open—an elevator. The two stepped in, nodding at the beggar in sync as he muttered, "See ya," right before the entrance slammed shut.

The elevator descended deep underground, stopping at level six. The digital display showed six more floors to go. On their way down, they exchanged hushed words. They had failed to locate their target.

"It's your freaking fault. We could've taken him out when we had the chance."

"Take a chill pill. We still got this covered."

"Tell that to Shorty when he finds out..."

"I got a plan."

"Hell right. It better be a good one."

"It'll stick. You'll tell him we've located his brother, that he'll lead us to him."

"That's not gonna stick."

"It will, I swear. Just tell him."

"No... you tell him."

The elevator came to a halt.

They stepped out into a hallway, glass walls on both sides filled with pharmaceutical logos. Beyond them, workers on a conveyor belt wrapped and bagged products in various forms—sachets, capsules, tablets—all moving in a symphony of machined precision. These products had to be manufactured underground. The man who owned it all was a maniac CEO with a lot of agency folks on his payroll. But as long as he stayed in his lane, they left him alone. The duo walked past a department where substances were synthesized into liquid form and fitted into beverages with big-name labels, all prepped for a chartered flight across the Caribbean.

There was a rugged staircase running down, covered in purple tapestry. The rug trailed along, stopping short at a lavish dining table where a man in a gray suit sat, sipping an Old Fashioned with orange bitters while scrolling through his phone.

He pulled out a thick wrap of stronger tobacco, exhaling a few rings before smiling at the two women. He waved them over. "I'm listening," he said.

The two exchanged glances before the one who had missed the hit spoke.

"We may have found him."

The man took another sip, his movements precise as he crafted his next drink—pouring the citrus and bitters, then gradually mixing bourbon and torching the rind with zen-like perfection.

"Didn't hear that. Come again."

The woman swallowed, nodding slightly. "We... we may have found him."

"May? Did I hear that correctly? You got him?"

"We've tracked down a relative—"

"How's that my freaking business? Don't freaking bore me. Did you or did you not find him?"

"We may have—"

"Don't freaking 'may' me."

"We—"

He sipped his drink midway, turning to the one who had spoken.

"Now, that's the kind of news I want to hear... Where is he?"

"We don't exactly know, but we have someone who will lead us to him."

"You see that?" He turned to the first woman. "That's how you talk. I should've hit you instead of her, you dimwit."

"What's his relationship with this 'someone'?" he pressed.

"A... a lover."

"Excellent." He grinned. "Now, that's the kind of result I'm looking for. It's just perfect."

The first woman stepped forward. "When do we bring her in—"

"All I want is my money. If she don't lead you nowhere, or you find him and he's acting funny, you know what you gotta do. Ain't that right, Nina?"

"Certainly." Both women chorused.

They vanished as quickly as they had come, marching off in sync. As they walked past the pharmaceutical glass walls, they stole a glance before stepping into the elevator.

* * *

January 2, 2020, Chicago

Leisha was in the lab with an awkward male lab assistant, who reportedly was hired a day ago, both of them poring over the records. Male Lab assistants wore white lab coats and black helmets, while Female associates wore yellow lab coats and orange helmets. Somehow, the only existing record of Mr. A's brain data was missing. As she pondered the possibility, only one person had access to it. She sank into her chair, her knees suddenly weak. The question was no longer who did it, but why.

"Why would she do it?" she whispered as the assistant ran further searches.

"Can we get the specific time it was retrieved from safekeeping?"

"There was never a record of it leaving the lab. We found out it went missing around ten last night. There's no video record of anyone ever going in there—"

"You mean someone wiped the CCTV system?"

"No, you've got it all wrong, Leisha. Have a look."

Leisha glanced at the screen. The monitor displayed various footage of the safe in Lab B41, dating back to the day Dr. X had placed it there for safekeeping. No one had entered since.

"Don't you find it strange? No one passed through the lab all that time—not even once. Isn't it possible the system was bugged, that the CCTV is just looping a scene?"

"No, Leisha. Our CCTV system is hackproof, so that's out of the question. There could only be one possibility."

Leisha found herself nodding, surprised the words left her own lips.

"Dr. X never kept the original there."

Just then, the lights went out, and the alarm system blared. Leisha raced for the door, but he stopped her.

"Are you crazy?"

"I've gotta tell James."

"It's not safe! You could get caught in the crossfire."

"I don't care!"

"I do! You can't go—"

Leisha struck him in the groin, and he staggered backward. She forced the door open, but as it creaked, something held her back.

"Let go of me, you pervert!" She rammed her foot into his face, hitting his neck in the process. She fumbled with the door, desperate to tear it apart, but it was sealed. Total lockdown.

When she glanced down, her heart skipped a beat. He was convulsing, his hands going stiff.

"No, no, no, no, no..." She felt for his neck. Something wasn't right. The thought made her heart scream. He needed air.

She undid his overall, unbuttoning his shirt. Then she noticed something—there was a lump on his chest. No, two lumps. His neck was also padded with some sort of layer. She pulled at it, and to her horror, it came off. It was a mask. Staring back at her, struggling for breath, was Dr. X.

* * *

Abhi felt as if he had been lost in a dream. And in that dream, his father had spoken to him. It was a recreation of what had happened in Calcutta that December of 1999. He had been playing in the garden while it rained, the scent of water mixing with the green of the grass, while the aroma of his auntie's cooking filled the entire backyard.

"Abhi!" his mother yelled. She rebuked him when he dried himself off. His father stood in the doorway, smiling.

"You won't say anything?" Sumati raged, casting him a nasty look before storming off to the kitchen. Anurag walked up to his son, running a hand through his hair.

"Mom gets angry a lot," young Abhi said.

"Don't talk about your mother that way." He pulled him close, straightening his son's collar. "You think your mom gets angry?"

Abhi nodded. "You do too. That's why I don't like old people. I don't want to be an adult. I want to be young forever."

"Are you sure that's wise? Because I don't think so. And you will not talk about your mother like that."

Anurag disciplined his son, immediately regretting it. Abhi's face crumpled, and he dashed off into the rain.

"Come back here… Abhi! Abhi!"

But he was gone.

That was the last time Abhi saw his father.

In the dream, Abhi had wiped his eyes clean in the attic where he hid, watching his father drive away. That was the last thing he remembered of him.

But something happened. Something that wasn't right.

As the young Abhi sat there, weeping, he heard footsteps—the sound of footsteps against the backdrop of rain crashing against stones. Footsteps. Closer. Closer.

Close.

"Abhi…"

When he lifted his head, he was no longer a kid. The garden, the penthouse, and the rain had long bled out of his field of vision. There was only blackness. Infinite blackness. And that voice…

"Abhi..."

A low-pitched voice, edged with an affection beyond what words could dictate. His heart raced, and his teeth chattered when he heard it. It had been over twenty years since he had last heard it.

"Abhi…"

His eyes welled up as he spoke.

"D—Dad."

In the black void—in that space of his subconscious—Abhi met his father. Not physically, at least. But he could feel him. His aura. His presence. He could feel his smile spreading over those thick lips. He could smell him. Abhi's feet trembled, and he wept.

"You're not here," Abhi said.

"I'm not. But I am somewhere else…"

Abhi swallowed. "Heaven…"

A chuckle. "Haha. Your heart. I've been here all along. I'm sorry it took this long for you to find me."

Abhi's eyes watered. Hearing his father chuckle sent waves of goosebumps across his skin. He wanted to laugh and cry. To scream and to stay silent. He wanted to fall to his knees, but something held him up. A hand. It wasn't really there, yet he knew it was his old man's, resting on his elbow, helping him stand.

"I'm s… I'm sorry…" Abhi choked out, water spilling from his nostrils as he struggled for words.

"Don't be… I've missed you more than you know. It was my fault. I should never have hit you. I'm sorry."

Abhi felt his father's arm on his shoulder—light yet heavy.

"You may think you're weird, that you're different, that you have no power. But that's not true…"

"What are you saying…?"

"I don't have much time. Listen... You feel awkward, not because something is wrong with you. All these years, you've meditated and beaten yourself up for things you didn't do..."

Abhi inhaled sharply, those words reverberating deep inside him. They hit hard.

"You feel awkward because what lies within you was too much to contain. But that was the past. Let the past be the past and hold on to the present."

Abhi shook his head. "I can't... I fear it'll destroy me. It's stronger, Dad... it's... it's stronger."

In that moment, flashes of past mistakes flooded Abhi's mind—beating up a kid at school, wrecking his father's car when he was five. And a more recent one—nearly killing the husband of someone he cared for. She had been too afraid to look him in the eyes. And though she told the cops he had saved her, her words never stopped haunting him.

"You're a monster..." she had said at the café where he had called her, right before she walked out into the daylight—out of his life.

Abhi let the thought fade.

"I can't... Dad, I can't..."

"That which you bury deep inside—you must let go. It is your light that frightens you most, not your darkness... Wake up, son..." His father's voice merged with the silence, echoing.

"Wake up, son..."

"Wake up..."

* * *

January 2, 2020, midnight, James' research facility

James watched from the other side of the glass, satisfied that his latest asset was about to be mined. It was a good thing they had discovered his abilities when they did. Remarkable things took time to harvest, and all that effort was about to bear fruit.

Anurag had left him some great assets, James chuckled to himself. He turned his back to the team, grateful for everything he and Dr. X had accomplished. All he had to do now was make sure she didn't blabber elsewhere.

The squeaks behind him grew louder, grating on his nerves. He found it irritating that a man like Abhi would cry over being injected. Even his sister hadn't shed a tear from those harmless injections.

"Can someone keep that man quiet?" James said, turning. But as his gaze fixed on the glass, his pupils shook.

"What… what in heaven's name is going on?"

Chapter 22

When Abhi opened his eyes, he was in Delhi, in front of their old house, a place he considered a safe haven. But it was completely deserted, and the night was dark. He couldn't think of anything, so he shouted out loud again, like flipping TV channels with a remote.

He was greeted by an intense beam of light right above his head. There were people around him—men and women dressed in white. Scientists. He tried to get up but couldn't. His arms and legs were locked away, sealed in metal casts. He tried to speak, but he couldn't scream anymore—whatever he was saying was foreign because these people hardly blinked, carrying on with preparing a machine that, he suspected, was taking him to his grave.

Somehow, Abhi gradually began to understand what was happening. He knew they were after his abilities, something he had just discovered how to harness. They wanted to take it from him. He knew this, but he had no idea how.

"Let me go! Let me go!" he started yelling in English. But no matter how hard he tried, his voice wouldn't rise—he must have been given something that had numbed his vocal cords.

He looked around and tried to wiggle, then turned sideways from his sleeping position. The floor hit him hard in the face. He was down, growling as his vision blurred.

Then, a voice crept into his head—a voice he knew too well, one he had heard over the years, over and over. It kept coming back.

It was Mary's voice.

You're a monster!

It kept coming back. He tried to stand, but his limbs weakened, a thousand hands overpowering him. He shook his head, trying to make it stop.

You're a monster… you're a monster… you're a mon—

Abhi's knees bled as they dragged him, throwing him over the machine. More hands rammed him down as they attached a gear to his head.

You must let go…

A seething agony tore through his skull as the machine hummed, a tiny beam of light coming to rest on his head, expanding as it grew awfully hot. The floor rocked violently as he fought to break free from the hold of his aggressors.

It is your light that frightens you… not your darkness…

He could almost feel his brain cells shifting as the scientists yelled at each other in a calm frenzy—the extraction was on. Abhi's pupils dimmed, everything reducing to a blur as his heart slowed to a pulse, darkness crashing hard on him. He was no longer moving.

The entire room fell silent, the only sound coming from the machine as it worked on the body, gathering bits of psychic energy from him. Abhi's mind was a blank slate now. Just as it would be when he woke up… if he ever did.

James stared at him, relieved that the anomaly had been brief. But he was in for a wilder shock…

There were words echoing around Abhi. Inaudible words. They kept coming back. From the darkness, spreading energy from mind to cells, to heart… they kept coming back… echoes…

Wake up, son…

Wake up, son…

Wake up.

Abhi's eyes lit up.

"Arrrrghhh!"

He sat up and cleared away the cobweb of wires around him. A fleet of guards flew off. The glass walls shattered, raining transparent debris on every piece of hardware and human in the room.

Abhi's voice was back.

He vanished—then reappeared. He felt... taller. The entire place was turned upside down, scientists racing off as firepower exploded around him. Nobody could rightly locate him—he was here one moment, and the next, he was sitting on top of the fridge.

Pfff!

One of the guards shrieked as Abhi dug his hand into the air. The guard's lips quivered.

"H-he caught a bullet."

Abhi gazed at his hand. There was no bullet.

"Happy New Year," he said, his voice deeply inhuman.

When Abhi blinked, stacks of data started compiling in his head. One of the guards stormed toward him with a taser. The guard had a bad knee and a liver issue—Abhi had picked all this up in a trillionth of a second.

When the hit came, Abhi simply stepped aside, the guard staggering into the extraction machine with a loud crash. Other guards started to circle him.

It was going to be quite a fight, Abhi thought, eyeing the weapons they began to pull out. Although their faces raged with cold confidence, their heartbeats were ticking bombs.

Fast as they ran, Abhi saw their every move like a movie in slow motion. He felt his blood rush, a sinister grin spreading across his face as he readied his fist.

Right then, Abhi dropped his fists, clutching his ears. Something was screaming in his subconscious. He could sense it—a woman's voice. It felt real. The screams. Like some sort of personal connection. Someone was in agony.

His heart raced as he glanced around, seeing through his incoming assailants and the series of walls and doors surrounding the facility. He sensed a heavy beam radiating somewhere deep inside.

He yelled when he saw it. The guards reached for him, pounding hard, a black wind swirling as they tried to stop him. When they stopped—he was gone again. Vanished. The only proof of his presence was the echo of what he had been yelling.

"Chandra!"

Chapter 23

Karan remained seated in the lounge of Legacy Inc, which seemed to be a two floor modern building.

Must have been designed by an architect, with strong passion for glass and steel.

He had been there for a while now, yet no one had attended to him. He took his time to observe the expansive structure housed behind walls layered with posh décor. There was nothing here—nothing to be found or studied.

He flipped the access card they had given him upon arrival. It was for 'special guests,' they had said—a special treat following the meeting. They had offered him coffee while he waited, but he had declined. Their 'special guest' had now been left unattended for what felt like hours. Karan composed himself, flicking the access card from finger to finger, inhaling the cold air.

"Karan Roy," a woman's voice called.

Karan lifted his head, relieved that the long wait was over.

"Happy New Year, sir! Our apologies for the delay—there was an unexpected occurrence."

"It's okay. Shall we proceed?"

"I'm afraid not, sir."

Those words struck Karan like knife blows. He cleared his throat. "I don't understand."

"Your meeting has been canceled…"

"May I understand why?" Karan stood there, flustered, checking the address on his phone's email.

"We apologize. The meeting had to be rescheduled.... Possibly tomorrow—that would be most suitable, I hope..."

"This is preposterous."

"We apologize. The error is on our part. We promise to make up for it."

"Thank you," Karan said, bolting toward the door.

He slammed his car door shut as he got inside, his grip tightening around the wheel.

Damn it.

He leaned forward, glancing into the rearview mirror. "Did you see all that?"

"I did," a voice chirped in his ear.

Not too far from where he was parked, a black vehicle was hidden behind a dumpster truck. Seated on the trunk was a woman wearing sunglasses with a sling bag on her shoulder, sipping a smoothie. Her eyes were glued to a tourist paper. Gloria was seeing everything Karan was seeing—she had been disguised as a tourist the entire time he waited inside.

"Did you run a check on the floors?" Karan asked, pulling off his eye contacts that had recorded everything he had seen, transmitting it to a device the size of a brick tucked safely in Gloria's sling bag.

"Cool down, Rambo. That's not how these things work," Gloria said, gliding her hand over the screen disguised as a tourist guidebook. She was running scans on the employees Karan had seen. So far, no one matched the profiles of who they were looking for.

At least it was some comfort to Karan that his father wasn't the major culprit in this hunt. Instead, they were after a man named James—James Barnes, the COO of this firm, who apparently lived here. Yet everyone had been fed the lie that he was visiting Manila.

"He's not in here," Gloria declared.

"Are you sure?"

"What do you want me to say, Karan? We can't get our eyes deeper..."

"Did you say deeper?"

"Yeah. What've you got on your mind?"

"It's just that I noticed something... about the floors," Karan said, rubbing his nose.

"What did you see?"

Karan glanced up through his windshield, his gaze climbing the building. The elevator. There was something about the elevator. Luckily, the front wall of the building was made of solid glass, making it possible for him to see what was going on inside. Anyone farther away—like Gloria, for instance—would have a hard time taking a peek without binoculars.

"What did you see, Karan?" Gloria's voice rose.

"The elevators... they go deeper."

"I'm not sure I'm following. Could you be more specific? We need to get out of here quick—I don't want to draw eyes."

"Wait." Karan climbed out of the car.

"Jeez, man, what are you doing?" Gloria yelled over the phone, but Karan was already out, storming toward the building while pretending to be on a call.

"The elevators... they run deeper..." he was saying. "There's an underground facility, Gloria. They have an underground facility!"

The line went silent, and Karan could guess Gloria was starting to see his point.

"Karan," Gloria's voice churned, "how on earth does that concern the task...?"

"They have something down there. That man, James—he's down there. You've gotta believe me..."

More silence on the line.

"First thing, Karan, there are several corporate buildings around town, and they all have underground facilities…"

"Listen, Gloria—"

"No, you listen! Listen, Karan!"

Karan quieted, the phone still pressed to his ear as he played the part of an agitated guest, his eyes sweeping through the front desk of Legacy Inc. He could see her—the woman who had asked him to come back. She was walking briskly, yelling over the phone. The employees were running around. Something was up…

"Are you listening?" Gloria's voice cut in.

"Yeah, yeah, I get it. I can't go in…"

"No, you can't. You'll be jeopardizing the mission by walking in without a legitimate reason. We've got to report to Stein."

"Did you just say legit reason?"

"What's on your mind?"

Karan reached into his pocket.

"I still have an access card to their lounge."

He hurried through the glass doors, making sure to avoid being seen by the lady.

When Stein had asked earlier how Karan found them, he had come up with a lie. He had claimed he carried a tracker and recorded the coordinates. But that wasn't true. Karan had a dream. And in that dream, he saw everything. It was like a trance, as if some divine entity was showing him a movie of what was going to happen. Who on earth would believe him?

He turned left, heading toward a pathway marked *Exquisite Suite.* A guard stood blocking the way, shaking his head as Karan approached.

"I'm afraid you can't come in now, sir…"

Karan flaunted the card. "I'm a guest. Here's my access card—"

"I'm sorry, sir, now's a bad time. Please exit the building…"

"Are you ordering me to—"

"Please, sir. I could lose my job…" the man said politely.

Karan strolled out of the building, his shoulders slumped. He was heading toward his car when he heard the roaring of engines. Seconds later, about ten vehicles crammed around the facility, men with tattoos and piercings jumping out and racing toward him.

Karan felt his heart squeeze, his feet failing to move.

"Gloria… Gloria, what's going on?! Gloria!"

He shut his eyes as they came, his hands clenched into fists. If he was going down, he was going down fighting.

To his surprise, though, they ignored him entirely. The men rushed past him, hardly sparing him a glance. Karan turned back and saw them disappear through the doorway, heading straight for the section marked *Exquisite Suite.*

Air crashed into his lungs as he leaned against a nearby car, gasping.

"...Do you copy?! Karan!"

"Gloria!"

"Thank God! Are you alright?"

"What the hell, Gloria?! I almost got lynched!"

"I had to take cover. One look from those guys and our cover's blown."

"No shit! Easy for you to say when it's my neck on the line."

"Hey, I was trying to warn you—"

"I yelled your name! You weren't answering—"

"The walkie-talkies were out of range. A hundred yards, remember? Anything more and the connection breaks," Gloria said.

Karan had been expecting an apology, and he was disappointed.

"We should head back. Hop in the car—" Gloria started.

"Something's up in there, Gloria. Something big. He's down there. James."

Silence. Gloria hesitated.

"Stein told you…"

"No."

"Then how on earth do you know it's him?"

"You wouldn't believe me if I told you."

Karan's gaze landed on a janitor slipping out of Legacy Inc. through the back door.

"Don't play games with me, Karan. This is serious. Are you a double agent?"

"Hell no. It's complicated."

"I'm listening."

"I found out… in a dream."

Silence.

"I told you—you wouldn't believe me."

"I'm calling Stein. You're compromised."

"Yeah? How else do you think I knew where your office was?"

Karan strolled toward the back door where he'd seen the janitor exit, his heart pounding.

"Karan…" Gloria's voice was careful. "Do you have abilities?"

Karan slipped inside.

He raced down a dark corridor, leaping down flights of stairs. Then—*déjà vu.* A flash. Voices. A woman's voice. She was weeping.

Somewhat disturbed, he pressed forward, relieved he had finally ditched Gloria. He was getting tired of her babysitting him. The moment he crossed through that back door, he'd exceeded the hundred-yard range needed for their electronics to work.

The connected contact lenses also stopped working. Without them, he had no access to the schematics of the building—no way to transmit his progress to the team. If this turned out well.

He landed hard, nearly tripping. He braced himself. The déjà vu deepened. He'd been here before—down this corridor. Maybe in a dream. Then he spotted it.

An elevator. He slammed his palm against the button.

Access denied.

Karan hit it again. Harder.

Access denied.

He frowned as he leaned forward, to read the signs. In the darkness, Karan saw the red glow of the sensor. He also made out the card symbol with the word SWIPE emblazoned beneath it. Quickly, he dug into his pocket and produced the access card. He swiped.

Unidentified personnel. Contacting head of security immediately.

"Damn it…" Karan muttered as the door behind him swung open. He swerved left, throwing himself into what seemed like a wardrobe. He heard footsteps—men mumbling as they drew near. The wardrobe was full of similar looking clothes – folded clothes on the floor and then hanging clothes; he pulled them around himself, quickly putting on the cleanest one he could find. But the men didn't come for him. They stood in a line before the elevator, chattering. They were talking about a Netflix show and they were not even talking in English.

Karan's jaw slackened as he read the display. Then, in the dim light, he noticed something else. The men were janitors. And they were heading down. He glanced at the stacks of clothes he was buried in.

Janitor uniforms.

When the elevator arrived, the workers filed in. At the last moment, someone who hadn't been with them suddenly sprang forward.

"Sorry, thank you," the worker mumbled as they held the door for him. He kept silent as they chattered on, his eyes locked on the button pad. Karan's heart started pounding faster when he noticed the number of levels below.

"Legacy Inc. is sitting on forty floors and not just the two floors."

Chapter 24

Outside, Gloria was back in her car, slamming the horn. She dialed her phone. A few rings later—

"I'm listening..."

"He's gone, sir. He bailed out on us."

She heard Stein excuse himself from a meeting. His voice returned. "What the hell went down there?"

"He knows something... he knows about Barnes."

"How's that possible?"

"I don't know. Thought he was a double agent until he told me how he did it."

"How?"

Gloria told him. She also mentioned that Karan had raced into the building.

"That doesn't make sense. One moment."

Gloria heard the line click as Stein made calls to confirm. Seconds later, Stein called back.

"Gloria, I need you to listen to me... carefully..."

Gloria sat up at the wheel, her phone stuck to her ear.

"Do everything in your power... everything... to make sure you get him out of there..."

"What're you saying?"

"Get him out of there... now!"

Seconds later, Gloria got the full update on Karan's background, her jaw dropping.

Karan parted from the team immediately as the elevator swung open. From the bit of chatter among the workers, he picked up on what was going on. Something had gone awfully wrong down there.

He found it a bit funny that those cleaning men had the word SWEEP scrawled on their vests. After all, these were the real guys doing the real cleanup down there. But as he trudged through the corridors and hollow paths alone, he had no idea what he was doing. He just knew he had to keep going. He just knew it.

He felt painfully stupid following his intuition this blindly. Priya would know what to do if she were here. Funny thing was, she had an interview this morning. Karan had left her with a kiss on the cheek while the day was still dark. He, Stein, and Gloria were going to have a lot of planning to do. And now, looking back, he wished he had spent more time with her. Loved her more. Been with her more.

This could be the end for him.

This giant building could come crashing down on him, and Priya wouldn't even know. He could vanish, just like Anurag—without a trace.

Karan's eyes were moist when he found a door. He wiped his face with his sleeve and immediately regretted it—he was still in the janitor's overalls. But he would take it off later, he thought, as his intuition pushed him to press through the door.

He did.

And then—he stopped.

He took a step back. Then two.

There were dogs in there.

Large, monster-sized dogs.

No doubt ferocious.

Karan didn't care to find out whether his assumption about their size was exaggerated because the moment he heard the growl, his flight instincts took over.

He stopped.

He could hear a hum. A song. A slow Indian song that was... Karan strode forward, clenching tightly to the pocket-sized shovel he had picked up from the janitorial wardrobe. Someone was there, singing softly as the two wild dogs growled.

His heart was making quantum leaps as he drew near, the voice growing clearer. He knew that song. He knew that voice. As he got closer, bile built up in his throat. And then—those eyes saw him. Eyes that had always welcomed him home with joy. A joy that had given him purpose all these years.

Karan's lips cracked open.

"M... Mom?"

* * *

Abhi raced toward the warm hue in his line of vision. The entire facility was a red fog. He ran with all his might, crashing through walls as the faint but distressed voice kept calling him back. He reached an elevator and tried to use it. Sealed off. Total lockdown. Through the button pad, he could see the chips—components he could reach into, tamper with, unlock the elevator. Abhi staggered, bumping into the metal doors. Then he saw them. They were coming. All of them. Twenty-six. The first man was heavyset, a badass biker tattoo stretched across his arm. Whatever it meant, Abhi knew it couldn't be good.

Bwaaah!

A beam of light exploded as shards of metal tore from the elevator. The structure collapsed on Abhi. They lifted one of the fallen walls—and to their horror, there was nothing underneath.

"Looking for me?" Abhi's voice chimed from above. They barely had time to react. "Happy New Year." Suddenly, they were flying—slamming into glass walls, their bodies rag-dolling midair.

The others shrieked at the sight. Abhi stood before them. The men scrambled, bringing out all they had. Firing.

Abhi watched the weird bullets speed toward him. He didn't move. From his view, time slowed to a crawl. He grinned, savoring the moment. The deadly allure of having such inhuman abilities. He was going to destroy these bastards for taking everything away from him.

* * *

Leisha unbuttoned Dr. X's overall, running a hand over her neck. Something was wrong. She had stopped convulsing but was having some sort of seizure. A panic attack, Leisha suspected. By reflex, she stormed toward a cabinet. She needed her pills. She ransacked the entire place, but there were none. The rest of the pills were stashed in a lab a few blocks away, but she couldn't get there—the doors had been sealed. Total lockdown.

"Stay with me, Doctor... stay with me..."

"Lei—Leisha..."

"Hang in there, Dr.... we'll be out in no time, hang in there... we'll be out... soon, pretty soon..."

"Listen... Leisha..."

Leisha held on to her, nodding fast as she watched hot tears rolling down Dr. X's cheeks.

"James... you can't... can't trust James..." Dr. X managed to say. "No one... no one survives extraction..."

"What're you talking about?"

"It's... all a sham, Leisha. God, I should've told you. It's all a sham. No one recovers after extraction. It's... it's imperfect..."

With strained effort, Dr. X told her the truth about extraction.

Leisha's mouth hung open as she listened to her mentor, her role model. It was a strange thing most people on the floor never saw or experienced, first hand.

"Extraction doesn't work the way it was designed—people die?"

Dr. X nodded weakly. "No one... no one comes out alive."

Those sentences hammered down Leisha's stern ethical walls. She was shaken as the truth about their work at the facility caught her off guard. All this time, she had believed she had joined the research program to aid humanity. It was supposed to help people with disabilities. James had said they were treating people with psychic symptoms, helping patients with disabilities, making the world a better place. He had told them they were extracting their illness, reprogramming their subconscious to compensate for their disabilities. Inside-out recovery, he had called it. She had even come up with better terms for it—psycho-medicines, neo-medicine, or, for the layman, heightened self-repair. It was meant to revolutionize healthcare, a novel way of treatment.

James had insisted their research be kept within these walls. But now, Leisha saw the writing on the walls. She saw where it led. And she was stunned by how gullible she had been. It had never even occurred to her that she had never seen a real survivor of the procedure. Not one.

"B-but... but... Mr. A... we have various video footage of him following his recovery... he was even drinking at a bar after extraction..."

"Made up... visual edits... it's all a sham, Leisha. A hoax. I'm... I'm sorry, Leisha... I couldn't tell you sooner... I'm sorry..."

"So... Mr. A never underwent full extraction...?" Leisha asked, dread creeping up her spine.

Dr. X shook her head. And the weight of that simple gesture drove Leisha to tears.

"It... it was my fault, what happened to him..." Dr. X admitted.

Dr. X glanced into Leisha's eyes and told her everything. Leisha had never seen Mr. A when he was brought in. At the time, James hadn't recruited her. Upon her recruitment, James had instructed Dr. X on exactly what to tell her new mentee. Together, they had fed her stories about the revolutionary healing method.

To make it real, they had fabricated video evidence, turning the supposed first successful extraction into a gripping documentary filled with highs and lows—machines malfunctioning, technical setbacks, tense moments of uncertainty. It was a deeply moving story. And at its climax, when a fully recovered Mr. A lifted a glass of wine, sipping it like any normal human would, Leisha had been convinced. That moment had cemented her dedication. She had been ready to spend the rest of her life at this facility. She would have given everything for it. And she wasn't alone—hundreds of other workers had been shown the same video, all of them convinced they were part of something groundbreaking.

Leisha shook her head as Dr. X finished speaking. So it had all been a hoax. A fabricated fantasy. Was that it?

"I don't believe you!" Leisha yelled, hands clamped over her ears. "It can't be... not true... not true..."

"It's my fault, Leisha... I should've told you..."

"How is this even possible? How?" Leisha screamed, her voice raw. "Answer me! How is it possible that we've been killing people... that you've been killing people all these years... how?" Her veins bulged as her fury surged.

"Yes... I... I hurt those people... It's my fault..." Dr. X's voice wavered. "We... we thought extraction was perfect. That it would work. But we were wrong... I was wrong—"

Right then, the door exploded, hot gas spilling into the mass of red hue that surrounded them. Leisha stepped backward, her eyes widening when she saw what lay beyond the door. She saw them—a glint of darkness. She could see it clearly as it walked through the door. It was a pair of eyes. Those eyes—they were dark. She watched the monster they had created, her knees buckling as she staggered backward, slowly raising her fist to ward him off. He was strolling toward them. He had his eyes on Dr. X.

"G… get away from her…" Leisha managed to say before he cast those eyes on her. She flinched, taking a step backward. She fell and passed out instantly.

Dr. X also lost her footing in the process and tripped, hitting her head on a desk.

Dr. X lay there, watching Abhi approach. She was in severe pain, her heart on the verge of breaking as the internal strains in her neck burned terribly. She had sustained injuries during her brief scuffle with Leisha, and now, staring at the monster of a man standing before her, she pulled back, trying to get away from him. His face drew near, and her skin crawled as those hellish eyes focused on her. Her nervous system was rippling, collapsing from the heavy stimuli his presence provoked. He knelt on one knee, eying Leisha's unconscious body, then sweeping his gaze back to her. She flinched as he brought his hand to her face. His eyes—there was something about them. It was then she saw it—the speck of white in them. This wasn't a monster… this was a human.

And those eyes reminded her of a man she had known—a man she had fallen for many years ago.

They had been at a museum, the two of them, watching rare species of sea creatures through glass walls when he kissed her. Her cheeks had burned when their lips met, a dark longing piercing the center of her thighs. It was a passionate kiss, as it was her first. Up until that day, and since her childhood, she had never kissed a man; she had never known one. And the memory of that moment would last her a lifetime. When they broke contact, she kissed him back, pressing her lips into his, longer... harder. She closed her eyes, savoring that moment. Even with her eyes shut, she could see his eyes—those awfully ethereal eyes of his.

"I swear to God," he had said, breathlessly, "you're beautiful..."

Her heart skipped at those words. He meant it. The glint in his eyes told her he meant it. He ran a hand over her face, and she wanted to kiss it... no, she did. She almost did. It was then she saw the faint mark on his finger. It was his left hand, the finger between his pinkie and the longest—his ring finger.

"You're married..." she said, stepping away. The glint in his eyes died, his face going ghost white. He glared at her, speechless for what must have felt like a thousand million years condensed into seconds. His lips parted slowly, and with some difficulty, he spoke.

"I'm married."

Smack!

She hit him in the face. She hit him so hard and stormed off, her eyes watering. He called after her, asking her to stop. He called her by her real name.

"Good God, Jenny, stop! Please stop, Jenny!"

And she wouldn't stop. She wept when she got to her apartment that night. She had loved him. She had genuinely loved Anurag.

* * *

Dr. X looked into Abhi's eyes, a tired grin spreading across her ace.

"You... you look just like him..."

Abhi glared at the woman, still unsure of what she meant. He didn't even know what he was doing. Earlier, he had heard screams in his subconscious— a woman's scream. And he had been led here. Somehow, he felt he knew this woman. She was bleeding—

internal bleeding. She was dying. Her name popped into his head: Jennifer. Jennifer Ximmer. She was also called Dr. X.

All the data he had gathered was now validated in his mind. He didn't know how, but it just came to him. He saw her name tag. It read Dr. Jenny X. Everything he was seeing was now confirmed true.

Abhi wanted to leave this woman. This was not Chandra. He had raced down here on the assumption that the distress call had been from his sister. He wanted to leave...

He couldn't.

This woman had known pain. And though she had played a role in his father's disappearance, she didn't deserve to die. For a moment, Abhi felt helpless, torn between two paths.

"Hang in there," he said, kneeling to lift her. She patted him, a wry smile spreading across her face.

"I'm glad... you made it, Abhi..."

Abhi had no idea what she meant. "Just stay quiet. I'll save you." He said, striding forward, her frame cradled in his arms.

"I'm... already... safe..." she said. With that final word, life slipped away from her.

Abhi watched, his pupils trembling as he checked her pulse. She was gone. Dead. He inhaled deeply, her lifeless eyes staring back at him. Gently, he closed them and laid her down with dignity. She was a courageous woman. She had known his father. She deserved better.

Better.

Abhi steadied himself and looked around. There was one more thing he had to do.

Chandra.

He had to find her. Not far away, the other scientist lay unconscious on the floor. Abhi checked her pulse—she was alive. She would be alright on her own. He moved toward the door but paused. Heavy footsteps. Those men were coming again. He focused hard, trying to sense Chandra's presence. He couldn't locate her. They had hidden her somewhere. Frowning, uncertain which way to go, he glanced at the still-unconscious scientist. She would know.

* * *

Karan managed to draw the attention of the wild dogs circling the chair where Sumati had been tied. The dogs growled, their jade-green eyes gleaming in the dim light. Slowly, the beasts began to follow him. His plan was working, though all he had was a vague idea of how to distract them. He had no clue what he'd do once they took the bait. But one thing kept him focused: the soft whimper that hissed out of Sumati's gagged mouth. It pushed him to keep going, more determined than ever to get her out of there. Right now, he wanted to strangle the bastards who had done this to his mother, but that could wait. First, he had two wild beasts to deal with. The dogs snarled, spittle dripping from their mouths as they followed him.

"Come here…there you go, boys, come…come…"

Seeing they were far from Sumati now, Karan broke into a sprint.

* * *

Chandra didn't know where she was. In her mind, she clung to the image of her father, one that had been stuck there ever since she saw him in that void. Something was wrong. Very wrong. That's what he had been telling her. And now, she could hear him. He was standing right next to her.

"Is this really you?" she asked, wondering if this was some crazy trick.

"No…but this is a part of me," her father replied.

"What have they done to you, Dad? And how can I talk to you… how?"

"Your accident has expanded your abilities. You no longer need to stare at photos to communicate with people. With someone's image in your mind, you can communicate with them…"

"I can only communicate with dead people…" Chandra murmured.

Her father nodded slowly. "You're much more than that. You can talk to anyone who is out of their body."

Chandra wanted to throw her arms around him, to hold him, to touch him. Her cheeks flushed.

"Where are you, Dad… what have they done to you?"

There was a moment of silence before Anurag spoke.

"Do you remember what I told you about the followers of Bama Khapa?"

Chandra studied her father, wondering what he was hinting at.

"You said a lot about Bama, Papa."

"That's true. Do you remember what I said about out-of-body meditation?"

Chandra's eyes widened. "You mean astral projection…"

"That's right."

"Yes… you said it was a safe spot, a complex experience you were trying to perfect."

"Don't forget, I also said there's a risk of getting lost in its worlds when the body is in a state of distress..."

Chandra's mind began to connect the dots. She glared at her dad, her mouth trembling.

"Dad…" she whispered, "are you stuck in another world?"

Anurag grinned at his daughter.

"That's my girl."

* * *

Outside Legacy Inc., Gloria leapt out of the car and ran toward the building, blending into the swarm of employees making their way out. She finally managed to slip through the glass door.

"I'm sorry, ma'am, I can't let you in. I could lose my job."

"Really?" Gloria lifted her shades.

He nodded.

Swish!

The man groaned as his body jerked backward, Gloria's knee driving into his groin while her hand struck a specific spot on his neck. He choked, collapsing to his knee, incapacitated.

"Tell your boss you got beat up trying to stop me." She stormed deeper into the now-empty building.

* * *

Abhi kept racing down a well-lit path with the girl on his shoulder. When he was certain he had put a good distance between himself and those guys, he set her down by a wall, taking his time to think and scan the next few floors. Still, there was no trace of Chandra. He gritted his teeth, a bolt of fear clawing at his chest. The things he would do if they hurt his sister. He could've easily stopped to confront the guys on his tail, but they knew nothing about Chandra. He shot his gaze back at the scientist and took note of her face. She was young—too young to have been in a place like this. She may have been an intern or a new employee. It was hard to tell, as she wasn't awake. He checked her name tag. Leisha. Leisha Lousse... he tried to pronounce her name. It sounded wrong. He gave up, his mind holding on to that first part: Leisha.

He shook her shoulders, willing her to wake. Nothing happened. He inhaled and tapped her lightly on the face. She hardly even budged. Furious, he slammed his fist into the wall. She woke up.

Abhi watched her recover, her gaze sweeping the area as if she had been in a trance all along. She flinched when she met his gaze.

"You can relax… I won't hurt you," Abhi said, "unless you make this a little too difficult."

What made it hardest was that he couldn't pick up Chandra's trail. Just like Dr. X's trail vanished…

What he needed right now were answers. And Leisha could possibly give him those. He only hoped he wouldn't have to push too hard.

"Please, don't hurt me…" she said.

"Chandra… where's Chandra?"

"I… I don't know who—what you're talking about. Please don't."

"Don't freaking play games with me. Where's she?"

"Sir, I don't know who Chandra is—"

"You're lying. Don't freaking lie to me, damn it!" Abhi drove his fist into the wall. She flinched as bits of debris poured from the impact. She hid behind her palm, whimpering. Abhi felt sorry for her. She looked hopeless, if not helpless. He rose, taking a few steps from her, and glanced back. His eyes blinked as he read her. A few pokes into her micro-gestures, and he knew she was telling the truth.

It then clicked. Even if she knew, he wasn't exactly making it easy for her. People tended to forget things during extreme situations.

"Listen…" he said. "The other girl—the one you were going to… extract…"

He hardly finished when her palms parted from her face. Abhi knew she now understood the girl he was talking about. She knew something.

"The... girl with the photographic delusion..."

"That's right," Abhi said, a bit confused by the misdescription. Chandra had no delusion. He hadn't yet figured out how Leisha had been fed an entirely different story about the people they operated on.

"Where is she? Tell me."

Her lips parted, quivering. "I... I don't know, sir."

"Don't lie to me... I swear to God I'll hurt you," he said through clenched teeth.

"I swear, sir, I swear... I don't know. Dr. X said they would have her moved somewhere. I swear to God, you've gotta believe me, I don't know... please, please, don't hurt me…"

Abhi unclenched his fist.

"Dr. X? You mean Dr. Jennifer Ximmer?"

She nodded. "How... do you know that name?"

Her tag. God damn it, Abhi didn't say. He ignored the question instead. Something else was on his mind. "Who else knows where they would've kept her... answer me!"

"James..." she sniffed. "James would know... but you could ask Dr. X, she's... she..." She looked around, puzzled. "She was here just now..."

Abhi's forehead furrowed. He couldn't blame her. She was still in shock. She hadn't processed the fact that they were no longer where he had found her. Abhi rose, his body aching.

"I'm sorry, Leisha," he said, his voice milder now. She saw his sudden calmness, and her face darkened, snot pouring down her face.

"What... what have you done to her?"

Chapter 25

The pounding of footsteps was followed by the snarling of dogs. Karan's breathless pace echoed up the stairs as he ran the 38 flights of stairs , entering a rusty bridge. At the end of the bridge was a door. Karan made for it, the dogs hot on his heels. His shirt was drenched with perspiration as he ran his hand along the railing, careful not to slip into the sewers below. He was almost at the door when his ankle got caught between a pair of canines. The dogs bit hard at his shoes, and he yelped as he crashed to the floor, his face pressed against the net-like metal of the bridge's floor. They tore at the thick fabric of his janitorial uniform.

Shrrrppp!

A tear appeared in the fabric below his knee. Karan pulled back, slamming his boot into the creature. The beast howled, baring its teeth. Karan saw it step back. But Karan had learned a few skills at the kennel club that he could apply. Only a couple of the dogs still had doubts about him, while the others seemed to have calmed down.

Bang!

One of the dogs dropped dead. The others fled the scene.

Karan was panting heavily when he lifted his head. Gloria stood in the doorway.

"Th-thank you…" he said, straining to get the dogs off of him. She joined him, helping him up.

"Thanks," he added, catching his breath.

Gloria stared at the two beasts, her gaze shifting to Karan. "We leave... now."

"There's someone I need to see..." Karan started to turn and leave. She grabbed his arm.

"Forget about Barnes—"

"It's not Barnes…" Karan interrupted.

Gloria's eyes hardened, her grip tightening around his overall. "You're coming with me, Karan."

"I've got to save my mother and..."

Gloria produced a cuff, snapped it around her wrist, and was about to cuff his hand when he slammed his head into her face. He cringed, staggering from the impact. She caught him, driving a hand to his throat. But Karan was quicker. He leapt backward, narrowly missing the fatal attack on his neck. Gloria flipped, throwing a boot into his face. There was a sickening crunch, and Karan fell backward, hitting the ground hard. He glanced up, finding her standing above him, her hand dangling with the cuff as she pulled him by his overall.

"You look pathetic, Karan," she said, finally clasping the metal around his wrist. She looked again—and suddenly, all she had in her hand was his dirty overall. Karan was already racing ahead.

"Seriously?"

She dashed after him.

* * *

Leisha was shaken.

God, she's really dead.

Dr. X had been like a sister to Leisha. A friend. Leisha never imagined it would come to this. Her death was something Leisha would need time to process.

"I know you're grieving, and I hate to ruin it…" Abhi said, "but if I don't get to my sister on time, she may end up like Dr. X... dead."

Leisha heard the anguished tone in his voice. She knew the girl he was talking about. Now that she understood they were running a slaughterhouse, not a health research facility, she recognized the urgency.

"I... I can help you find him..." Leisha said.

The man's gaze shot toward her, hope registering in his eyes.

"The man who took her... Barnes... I can help you locate him."

"I will take a life for you, Leisha..."

"I can't guarantee he'll be there, but... we could try," she sniffed. "He's always there two nights out of seven. He's always there when things get a little... mushy."

She struggled to stand as she spoke—she had hurt her ankle when she fell earlier. Abhi offered to help.

"No, I'm... I'm fine. I can get up..." Leisha said, slowly rising with her back against the wall. She made it only a few steps before crashing back down. Her ankle was killing her. She couldn't even manage to stand properly. There was also a deep ache somewhere in her kneecap. Without a word, the man picked her up, carrying her in his arms as he began walking into the red fog.

"My name is Abhi... and... I'm sorry I had to scare you," Abhi said to Leisha as he climbed the stairs that seemed to go on forever. She simply remained in his arms, her eyes scanning over his arms, chest, and form. He looked... unreal.

"I wasn't sure you could be trusted," he continued. Leisha's face was still shaken, her cheeks and eyelashes coated with dried tears. She remained silent, carefully listening to his words, to his ragged breath. His voice carried the tone of a troubled soldier.

"And I'm deeply sorry about Dr. X... she was a good woman. She must have been like a big sister to you..."

"More than that..."

"What did you say?" Abhi asked, lost in his own thoughts. He hadn't fully heard her words, or perhaps he had and simply wanted to hear her voice again.

"She was more than a sister… she was a friend… you could say she was the only friend I ever had."

Abhi pushed past more stairs, while getting to know Leisha. It felt strange how much Leisha had in common with his sister, Chandra. They were about the same age, and they truly believed that they were serving mankind. And they had both lost someone dear to them. Pierre had meant the world to Chandra. He was her only ray of hope, her only connection to the real world—a world outside the academic confines of dense textbooks on algorithms and psychoanalysis. Pierre was her redeeming feature. And he had been taken from her.

Abhi came to a halt. Leisha glared at him, wondering what was wrong. Had she done something wrong? But Abhi's mind was far from here. He was stretching his focus, turning his head sideways, listening intently to make sure his senses weren't misleading him.

Damn it.

In that moment, an ear-shattering explosion threw Abhi off balance. The walls tore apart, gigantic shards of shattered ceramic falling hard around him. He ducked just in time, as the floor split beneath him, preventing Leisha's face from taking the brunt of the blow. They both fell, crashing to the ground. The sound of walls collapsing, debris, and gunpowder filled the air.

The lights went out.

When Abhi opened his eyes, Leisha was on top of him, her face inches from his, their noses almost touching. He could see her heartbeat quicken. Suddenly, he became aware of her perfume. They both rose slowly, their gazes still locked.

* * *

Gloria raced after Karan, yelling at him to stop. But Karan wouldn't have it. He kept running. Gloria stopped, aiming her gun at him. She steadied her grip, inhaling deeply as she focused, her finger just inches from the trigger.

Karan vanished.

Gloria's brows shot up. She stared at the spot he had been standing, wide-eyed.

What in the world?

Gloria wondered why she felt so agitated. She had spent the bulk of her life scraping crumbs off the bottom of the food chain. She knew struggle. It was why she wasn't taking it easy on bastards who were handed everything without effort, all in the name of inheritance. "You earn your shit" was a motto that had shaped her. You win if you deserve it. You lose if you deserve it. It wasn't about fairness; it was about getting things done—failure after failure after failure. For all she knew, Karan might have been putting on a show the whole time. Maybe he even knew where his father was. Perhaps his company was just a front to push his father's totalitarian agenda.

In that instant, Karan was racing back toward her. She blinked, somewhat taken aback. He was yelling… yelling something.

"Run! Runnnnnnnn!"

Gloria readied her gun, standing still as she aimed at him. Her jaw dropped when she saw it. Racing after Karan were five greyhounds.

***

Their feet clanged hard as they raced, wild dogs on their tail. The duo pushed on, Gloria further ahead, her feet pounding the floor. They were racing back to the bridge where she had saved Karan.

"Slow down! Slow down!" Karan yelled. Gloria wondered what in the world that lunatic was talking about. She pushed on, ignoring his 'safety tips.' As she did, an awful crash rang out beneath her, and the net-like metal flooring of the bridge gave way. Gloria fell fast. She clawed at the edge, its sharp corners drawing blood from her flesh.

Clang, clang, clang, clang.

They were coming.

She could see Karan ahead, his feet slapping the ground clumsily as he ran, the green-eyed beasts behind him. The floor rocked as a thousand steps marched forward. Gloria gasped for air, the metal digging deeper into her skin. She was going to be mobbed—a stampede. They would rip her to pieces. She glared down at the abyss, a black hole extending deep, deep down. It went on forever, a gaping void—tempting her to take a leap of faith into its deadly depths.

A leap of death.

The dense, rancid smell of the sewers reached her nostrils, and her eyes clenched shut. This was going to be a rough one. She swallowed, cursing, her gaze locking on the advancing beasts. She was outnumbered—thousands against one. They were getting closer. Gloria took a deep breath. This was it. She was going to die. All her dreams, everything she held dear... none of it would matter in this one moment. She shut her eyes tightly. She would take that leap of faith. She would take it. She inhaled and whispered a short prayer. Silence.

Grip!

Something yanked at her vest. A hand. Gloria glanced up, her breath catching as she saw Karan standing at the edge, his grip tight around her vest.

"What... are you... doing?" he said through gritted teeth, pulling her back up. He collapsed to the floor when she was finally on her feet, gasping for air. Gloria stood there, wide-eyed, stunned. Had he just saved her life?

"You're welcome..." Karan said, still on the floor, breathing heavily. Her gaze flicked between him and the beasts. "They're mourning." These same creatures had been chasing him just moments ago.

"You find it funny?" Gloria shot back.

"Only heavens know what's really going on here," Karan muttered, looking around. "An invisible fence? It really is amazing."

"I suppose so—wait, where are you going?" Gloria called as he turned to leave.

"There's someone I need to see." Both of them took the elevators down to the floor where his Mom was locked up.

Gloria's heart twisted as she watched Karan embrace the woman. When he untied her, it hit Gloria like a punch to the gut. This was his mother. Good heavens, she thought. How long had she been kept here, guarded by wild dogs?

Karan was gently calming her mother now, his voice soothing as he wiped the tears from her frail face. The woman looked so weak, a shadow of whatever beauty she must have had before being trapped down here. Gloria felt a lump form in her throat, a sharp ache stabbing deep in her chest. She felt so small and humbled in this moment. Here she was, saved by the man she had once tried to capture.

What if she had succeeded? His mother would still be down here, rotting away.

Chapter 26

Leisha was still tugging at Abhi's arm. Abhi tried to stretch, but she fell into the dust. Panicking, he rushed to her side. She flinched when he drew near, hiding her gaze from his intense eyes.

Abhi heard those words again in his mind.

You're a monster…

…a monster.

He tore his gaze from her and turned to face the man waiting for him, hands spread for combat. The man rushed at Abhi, but Abhi didn't move. The moment the man lunged, Abhi grabbed his shirt, lifting him high. He inspected him, tilting his head, forehead creased. The man started choking before Abhi let him drop to the ground.

"I'm not letting you off that easy," the man growled, jumping onto Abhi's back and squeezing his arm around his neck. Abhi bent quickly, and the man fell off. The man produced a knife and aimed for Abhi's eye, but Abhi caught the blade, snapping it in his grip. He lifted the man and slammed him into the wall. The man stuck there like a living room art.

"Do yourself a favor…" Abhi glanced at him. "…never come back…"

With that, Abhi left.

* * *

"You're wounded…" Leisha said, following him since the fight, saying nothing else.

"I'm fine."

"It'll worsen…"

"I'm... fine…" Abhi replied, his eyes glinting. She feared him.

"Listen…" His voice wavered, trying to sound stern, unmoved. "It's best you go without me…get yourself out of this mess. Start your career fresh."

Leisha felt tears sting her eyes. But it was easier this way. Someone had died in his arms today. He had Chandra to worry about. Who knew what lay ahead.

"It's… it's okay…" she nodded, sniffing.

Abhi's eyes remained shut the entire time it took her to leave. He heard her feet scratch the floor as she limped. When he opened his eyes, the silence was deafening. Too quiet.

She was gone.

* * *

Karan, Sumati, and Gloria rushed out of the suite marked '*Exquisite Suite.*' The guard flinched when he saw Gloria.

"Thanks." She winked at him as he stared, startled, watching them leave. They piled into Karan's Mercedes. Tony had gotten the car's tires and windows repaired - a show of courtesy, when they had agreed to play as a team.

"I'm driving," Gloria said as Sumati sank into the backseat. Karan glared at her, his stern gaze cutting into her. He slid her the key and sat beside his mother. Sumati remained silent, her face pale and covered in dust. Karan's heart raced as the car roared to life.

"Where do we go?" Gloria asked, her gaze focused on them through the rearview mirror. Karan glanced at Sumati's face. It was drained, like a shadow of what she had once been. His heart raced again as he wondered what they had done to his mother.

"The hospital."

The Mercedes swerved around the corner, heading toward the main road. Karan felt a sense of foreboding, as if something was about to go wrong, but he quickly pushed the thought away. His mind was elsewhere.

Chandra and Abhi.

Heavens knew where they were. But he couldn't think about them now. His mind was too clogged. Sumati needed care—and then—

Kabooooshhhhhh!

The car spun violently as another vehicle slammed into them, glass shattering as the world spun around. When the car came to a stop, it hung upside down. Sumati's scream jolted Karan awake. Even through his blurred vision, her voice cut through the chaos. She was sobbing now, as they all hung in the wreckage. Through the shattered window, he saw the vehicle pull over. It was the black van he'd seen earlier, now wrecked at the front. Two pairs of feet jumped out, boots pounding the asphalt as they drew closer. They were clad in black leather pants and jackets. They stopped by the car. Karan saw their faces.

"Hello," Nina and Tina said.

* * *

Two Hours Later

Abhi sat in his cramped apartment, rummaging through the fridge. His appetite was monstrous. He wasn't surprised when he checked his call log and saw no call from Karan. But considering everything that had happened, he wasn't sure how long he could keep up with their zero-communication habit. He left the phone with the ringer on as he moved around, munching. He almost dropped a text message but hesitated. Priya might be home, and he didn't want to scare her with what had happened. Besides, if Karan hadn't told her, it wouldn't be right for her to hear it from him.

Abhi sank into his bed. He just needed to talk to someone. Anyone. He glared at the mirror, his face battered with bruises. He leaned closer to inspect the wound.

Suddenly, he spun, his heart racing. Someone was here at the door.

He dropped the piece of bread, threw on some clothes, and trudged to the door. It was the last person he expected to see.

Leisha.

"What are you doing here?"

Leisha stood in the doorway, still dressed in what she had been wearing earlier.

"I... I have nowhere else to go. They know where I live and all the hotels in this area."

Abhi stared at her, taking in the sight of her rumpled hair, her face a mix of beauty and mud. She still smelled nice.

He nodded, scanning the area. It was clear.

* * *

"What do you mean they vanished? How's that even possible?" Stein yelled into the phone.

"Find them. ...then make it happen!"

He ended the call, frustration evident in his voice, just as one of his men hurried in, holding a USB.

"What's that?"

"Video footage from the scene. You've got to see this, boss.

Stein stood, his hair still dishevelled from the news of Karan and Gloria's disappearance. The man began setting up the display. The footage ran for a while, showing a road just across from Legacy Inc., random strangers, and vehicles passing by.

"What kind of crap is this?" Stein's cold eyes narrowed.

The guy grabbed the remote and fast-forwarded it.

"Stop there... back it up a little."

The video reversed.

"Right there. Right there. Zoom in on that panel." Stein said, drawing near to the display with his arms folded. The image zoomed in, showing the rear view of a car.

"Is that our Mercedes?"

The guy nodded, his eyes glued to the screen. "I ran a check on it, it's the same number plate."

Everyone in the room watched as the car made a turn toward the exit when—

Bam!

The guy gasped. "Holy molly!"

Stein stared at the screen, confused. "What… what's that?"

He glanced around, realizing that his team had kept him in the dark.

"Who hit us? Who?!"

The guy scrambled for the remote, zooming in as the video continued. The frame now filled with the image of two women dashing out of the assaulting van. Stein squinted at them, cupping his chin.

"Who are they?"

"I'm running a check."

Minutes later, Stein received a print-out with every bit of detail they could find on the women.

"There's Nina and Tina," Socks said. "They work for Marcus Halls, a drug lord in the suburbs. They're his errand girls, handling his dirty work—cleaning out debts, paying annoying clients a 'friendly' visit."

"What's he got to do with our guy?" Stein asked. "Look, they go straight for him. They know him. Why? I need answers. Why would a drug dealer want Karan?"

"Still picking up the pieces."

"Well, pick harder. Someone's life is on the line here. Ortega's tracker went off the grid about two hours ago, okay? That's a problem. If this freaking Halls guy touches my agent, I swear, I'll have you picking scraps on the streets." The guy said nothing, his gaze still locked on the screen. He moved to eject the USB.

"Wait..." Stein said, his eyes snapping back to the screen. "Play that again... no... back it up a little. A little more. Yeah, there."

On the screen, a man was strolling out of the building. Stein leaned closer, his brows shooting up.

"Is that who we think it is?"

Chapter 27

Chandra's mouth fell wide open as she replayed what her father had revealed to her.

"Are you saying you're stuck, Dad? That you've been stuck in this astral state for…" Her voice croaked, "…twenty years?"

Anurag noticed the water drops on his daughter's face.

"How can we get you out? There's got to be something they can do to help."

"You are already helping. You should see Abhi though; he has finally discovered his powers."

Chandra paused, letting that sink in. "Abhi… powers?"

Anurag nodded, noticing the stifled excitement in her voice.

"Dad, we must get you out… How can we get you out? How can I see you?"

Anurag smiled. "You will see me… sooner than you expect."

* * *

Leisha scraped the bowl, downing every last bit of milk. Abhi watched her from where he sat and he shook his head in disbelief.

"You think you're the only one who's been pushed away? You think I asked for this? All I'm asking for is letting me stay here tonight, and you are so unsure - you're acting like a classic jerk. You know what, forget it. I'd rather just lie on that bridge and die."

She started walking away when he called her. She stopped, bits of raindrops hanging in the air. Abhi raced toward her, throwing a coat around her. Minutes later, they were in Abhi's kitchen, searching for food. Who would've believed that just moments ago, they had both hated each other's guts, that they had both faced death?

"My life... my life is ruined," she said. "I'm down here, talking to a stranger, getting high on… cereal... but she's still dead. Dr. X. She's still gone, and she… she's never coming back."

She sobbed.

Abhi waited patiently. He wanted to hold her, even for a moment, but he held back. When he felt she'd cried enough, he touched her hand.

Thud.

"What… who?"

Abhi turned and saw that the main entry door was open. He reached out to close it. Someone was there. His senses kicked in. The weather had improved now. He made his way to the sink, washing his hands and whistling as if nothing had happened.

"You know we're here, don't you?" The voice came from behind him. Abhi stopped for a moment before continuing to wash his hands, as if those words were just fiction from his imagination.

Surely, these clowns followed Leisha to get to me.

"We know where your brother is… where Chandra is…"

Abhi's head shot up at the mention of Chandra's name.

"Yes, and to top it off, your mother is with the party too."

"If you freaking lay your damned hands on Mom…"

"Chill, Abhi. We aren't the enemy. We've merely offered to help. Please, have a seat."

"I'm not sitting until I find them."

The man clapped his hands, and the door swung open. Another man entered, carrying someone. Abhi's eyes widened when he saw the person.

"I insist." The first stranger said. "Have a seat."

Abhi slowly sat on his bed.

"What do you want?"

* * *

"Technically, they're women, but yes. You know Halls?"

Abhi said nothing in response.

"Will you be squaring things up with Halls??"

Abhi gritted his teeth. Heaven knew he wouldn't be answering these questions if he were on his own. This was why he hated entanglements—things like this left you compromised. He stared at the man speaking, his eyes fixed on the sharp object in his hand, which was caressing the neck of the woman in the chair.

"I see you're taking your time, Abhi. Please, take your time. You have all the time in the world," the man whispered into her ear.

Abhi nodded quickly. "I... owe Halls some cash."

"How much? Cocaine money, huh?" the intruder asked, his partner sitting in a chair, watching them go back and forth while he ran a blade over the neck of the woman. Abhi saw her gentle eyes light up at the mention of coke. This wasn't going to go well, but he chose to evade the question.

"I needed it..." Abhi said, not caring about the thoughts running behind those eyes.

"Abhi, she's this close to taking a blow to the neck..." the man said. "Answers. I need direct answers. What did you need the money for? You're into drugs? I see those muscles bulging around your neck. You into steroids?"

"Answer me!" The man yelled, pressing the knife hard into Leisha's throat.

"God damn it, I needed it for Mom's surgery a while ago."

"I really hate to have come disturb you, Abhi." The man ran a knife through Leisha's hair, a tired, dry grin spreading across his face. "But we've got to know you're on our side."

"I'm not on anybody's side."

"If I were you, I'd choose my words wisely." The blade caressed Leisha's neck now.

"Whose side are you on, Abhi?"

Abhi swallowed. His vocal cords were still strained and may not work to get him his powers. Heaven knew he wanted to race toward this bastard and smack him so hard he'd lose his head, but Leisha would die in a moment. The other guy standing in the corner had a gun. He could take Leisha out in a heartbeat. Abhi kept running different scenarios in his mind of how to get her out of there without a scratch.

"I asked a question, Abhi. I hate to ask questions twice." The man was now drawing the knife over Leisha's thighs.

Abhi swallowed. "I… I'm on—"

Right then, Abhi's landline rang. The entire room fell silent as both men shot stares at each other while the phone's ring filled the air. The man rose, whispering into the ear of the man with the knife. For a moment, they engaged in a brief conversation.

The phone kept ringing.

The man with the knife finally said, "Pick it up…"

Abhi rose gently, his hands spread out.

"…And, boy," the man said, "…don't play games. Your Snow White here will have no life if you try anything stupid."

Click.

"Hello?"

"Thank goodness, Abhi… God, I've been so worried about you…"

"Priya…"

"Abhi, I can't find Karan. I've been trying his line, but it's not going through. Abhi, please help me find him—"

"Calm down, Priya." Abhi said, eyeing the men. "Karan is probably just out, taking his time…"

"Not recently, not since the litigation…"

"Litigation?"

"You didn't know?"

"Know what?"

Priya told him in one breath.

Abhi nodded as Priya finished speaking.

"Yeah, not to worry, I'll… I'll try and find Karan. Now, you get some rest, okay…

"C…can we meet… tonight…?"

"Now's a bad time, Priya. I'm sorry." Abhi said, glaring at the two men. "I'll call you when I've got news."

The call ended.

"Jeez, man, that was some crazy-ass woman. She your girlfriend?"

Abhi said nothing.

"Answer, boy, or I could just run a trace on that line and have my boys drop in on her…"

"If you dare lay a finger on Priya…"

"Girlfriend it is then… haha."

Abhi tried not to look at Leisha. He inhaled, his hands deep in his pockets. "Who are you guys, and what do you want?"

"It's pretty simple, Abhi. My partner here will enlighten you."

Just then the partner's phone rang and both of them left the room. Both Abhi and Leisha kept looking at each other, confused by the intrusion.

Soon thereafter the partner came back in and looked at Abhi – "Danny Boy, speak with my boss"

* * *

"Sir, we have a lead on James Barnes…"

"What? Where are they?" Stein dropped the file he was going through.

"Elgin… It's heavily guarded, but we can break in. We suspect he'll be trying to leave the country."

"We can't let that happen. You're heading to Elgin now. Take him down if you must. You can't let him get away."

"Will do, sir." The comrade said, motioning to leave.

"And Socks," Stein called. "Any news on them?"

* * *

As of seven o'clock, Abhi was in a van heading to an underground drug facility. He had called Halls. The conversation had been short.

"Halls—"

"Why you call me?"

"Halls, listen, there's been some misunderstanding—"

The line went dead.

Abhi looked out the window. Yeah, it had been a 'lengthy talk.'

"It's alright here." Abhi said, getting off the van. He had gotten off a good distance from Halls' HQ and started the long walk. All around him, there were junkies, bloodshot from whatever substance had become their staple diet. The streets were a mess—upturned trash cans, flies buzzing around as the smell of rot caused Abhi to hold his breath a little longer. Soon, he reached the metal door.

He banged six times.

The small rectangular-shaped window swung open, and a pair of eyes glared through the hole.

"What you want, Low Key?""

"The boss."

"Get lost, Low Key." The opening swung shut.

Abhi banged again. He kept banging, gritting his teeth, all while taking in the lay of the land. The place was a fortress. Freaking impregnable. Besides, he would hate to drop in unannounced. That would be extreme disrespect. Wall had been somewhat of a friend to him. They had met during his brief time in police custody. That's right—Abhi had been in police custody. For manslaughter. For holding George before George slipped and died.

Following that incident, Abhi had run. It was Mary's idea. He was scared.

"Run… run!" Mary had yelled as he stood, his blood-soaked body shivering as the thought of what he had just done sank into his subconscious.

"Get out of here!" Mary had said as the sirens drew close. Abhi had bolted. A few hours later, Abhi found himself behind bars, facing a likely death penalty for manslaughter. Mary had come through at Abhi's hearing. She had testified that Abhi had saved her, that George was going to kill her. Further evidence revealed that Mary had been the subject of domestic violence—health examinations, scars, tests, witnesses. Everything pointed to how much of a wife-beater George had been. In the end, the verdict tipped in Abhi's favor. Abhi had met up with Mary weeks after the hearing. That was when they had the conversation that would come to haunt Abhi for life.

Abhi shook the thought from his head, staring at the steel doors. Halls was watching him right now. He knew Halls was. Halls was facing life imprisonment. The two had mixed quite well. Halls often got bullied by the inmates. That's when they called him Shorty. Abhi had stood up for him—and gotten beat up. A few times. But jail life wasn't so bad after all. With Halls' connections, the boys were smuggling coke, weed, you name it, through a backdoor. Abhi had saved Halls from the prison cops when Halls was found with a cell phone. Eventually, all that drug money came in handy, especially when Halls finally acquired one of the most sought-after lawyers.

"The bastard's asking an arm and a leg," Halls had told him after they both got mugged again by some group of inmates. One of Halls' eyes had been purple. Abhi had a long cut on his face, both of them lying side by side on separate beds in the infirmary.

"Paid him anyway. By July, I'll be getting out of here."

And he did. It took two months before Mary's testimony came through, and when it did, Halls' men were waiting to collect Abhi. Halls had been that good to him. Halls only had one problem—his hardcore principles and rules. He followed them to the letter. He was notorious for it. He kept his word when it came to agreements, and he was patient. Very patient. His first rule: Don't ever lie to him.

And Abhi knew he had long crossed that line when he promised to pay up Halls' cash and had instead bailed on him.

Abhi waited outside, his back to the steel door. He would wait. Soon, he was on his butt, napping away while darkness crept through the clouds.

Smack!

Abhi jolted out of his sleep. When he glanced up, there was a gun barrel in his face.

"Get up."

* * *

Abhi was led into Halls' chamber. The air smelled unusually nice. Since when did Wall's room smell this good? Abhi was always greeted with the scent of some expensive cigar, tobacco, or weed—take your pick. The room was mostly cast in shadows. Abhi spotted a figure sitting at a dining table. Halls was there, dressed in a suit with his shirt loosely open. Abhi suppressed a grin. Halls didn't look bad in that suit.

"Sit your ass down," Halls said, retaining his composure as his men brought Abhi in. Abhi sat opposite to him.

"You've lost weight," Halls said, filling up two glasses with expensive single malt, his hand glistening with rings on each finger.

"I see you've grown taller," Abhi replied.

Halls was torching the orange peel over the second glass now. "I assume… you come to pay your debt…"

"About that… Halls, see, I think there's… there's been some misunderstanding," Abhi said, watching Halls grin as he filled the glass.

"You know what misunderstanding is?" Halls went on, filling the glass, "It's when you get something a lot…"

Abhi watched him fill the glass to the brim. It was overflowing now, single malt soaking into the table's exquisite fabric.

"…and you forget it's expensive," Halls finished, his steel-like eyes glaring at Abhi. Abhi nodded slowly.

"This…" Halls nodded at the soaked fabric, "this is expensive Scotch. You waste it. Like you waste my patience…"

"Halls, I know I made a mistake…"

"Nah… you didn't make a mistake, Habi… You screwed up big time! Like, major league screw-up…"

"I know, and I'm going to pay up. You have my word, but can we just talk about my brother and mother…"

"Now, why would I want to talk to you about your family?"

Abhi rubbed his chin. "I know… I know… you're mad, and I get it… but scooping my folks off the streets, that ain't your style, man…"

"What are you talking about, Habi?"

Abhi's forehead creased. "My brother and my mom…"

"What's up with them?"

"Don't play games with me, Halls..."

"Who the hell are you?" Halls' voice rose, in his Eastern European accent. "You come into my place, accuse me of..." and then he launched into a string of swear words.

Abhi glared at Halls, blinking. Halls knew nothing about his brother and mom. He cleared his throat.

"Your girls... where are they?"

"You ain't hearing anything until you tell me what this is all about..."

Abhi massaged his eyebrows, his gaze sweeping the entire space.

Minutes later, Nina and Tina entered. Halls glared at the two women, his eyes burning.

"Is it true?" Halls asked, his teeth clenching as he enunciated each syllable. "Is it... true?"

The girls nodded in agreement with Abhi.

"Where are they?"

One of them lifted her head and spoke. "At... at the warehouse..."

Halls nodded. "You hid them on my property? You're freaking hiding hostages on my property!"

Abhi watched Halls talk, veins bulging from his neck.

"Why'd you do this? Answer me or I'll smack that look off your face."

Just then, there were noises outside—the sound of gunfire.

Halls frowned, his gaze shooting towards the door. He grabbed a control on the table and hit its button. A display came alive, showing live CCTV footage of his front door. His eyes flared as he shot Abhi a look.

"You bring cops to my yard?"

* * *

James was prying through stacks of files, observing the girl in the chamber. They had arrived a few moments ago and found her weeping when they opened the van. He may have lost a lot back in Chicago, but she would fetch him everything he lost. He would make sure of that.

"How soon do we start?" he said to a man perched behind a microscope.

"One moment..." the man replied, "I'll be with you shortly..."

Finally, the man left his microscope-type apparatus, typing dexterously on a touch keyboard.

"It will only take a few hours. Three at most."

James grunted.

The man grinned, leaving the desk to stand next to him. James was much taller than him. And younger.

"I see you're still upset over our loss."

"If only I had kept a closer watch on him..."

"The past is past, James."

"I lost a lot of your money in that failure. You should be mad, not giving a compelling speech."

The man chuckled. "When you've lived through enough wars and economic meltdowns, failure becomes something to be expected. You do not run from failure, James. You embrace it. I need to go take a nap," the man said.

James watched his mentor leave the room. He was starting to find the man's unrelenting confidence annoying. But what could he do? Any regular boss would've fired or killed for the catastrophe back in Chicago, yet this man—this A.G. Griss is loving life and the course it is taking.

Was he a saint?

James returned his eyes to the display showing the chamber where they kept the girl. He left the room. Seconds later, just after he shut the door, a stealth team slowly crept through the fortress, the word "Tony's" emblazoned on their vests.

Chandra woke up. She didn't know where she was.

* * *

Outside Halls' building

"I thought we were meant to wait for his call," said the man with the scar on his face, the one who had held a knife to Leisha's neck earlier.

"Abhi's been gone too long. They've probably iced him."

"This is a bad idea."

"No, losing him and his brother would be a bad idea. You know how much he's worth on the market?" The man stared at the beggar they had gunned down, right at the door. The elevator swung open.

"Nice..." the scarred man said as they trudged in.

"When will the others be here?" his partner asked.

"They're already here."

Right then, dozens of cars roared as they parked, men in blue vests hurrying out and trudging into the place. Scarface grinned at his partner as the elevator doors shut.

Chapter 28

Halls had a gun pointed at Abhi.

"You brought cops to my place?"

"This wasn't the plan."

"Freaking shut up. I'm gonna blow your head off, alright?"

"Tina, get the car ready," Halls said, still the gun pointing at Abhi. "We're going for a ride."

They hurried through a back door just in time to hear gunfire erupt behind them. Nina and Tina raced forward while Halls' other men opened fire, leaving Halls and Abhi in the middle. Abhi thought he heard Chandra's voice in his head. She was saying something. Her words were faint. Really faint. But his ultra-sharp senses could pick it out amidst the chaos. Her words were simple:

I've found him...

Right then, Abhi felt a strong connection with Chandra and Karan. It was as though a strange thread of light descended on him, filling him with a presence outside this physical world. At that moment, he felt as though he could feel Chandra, Karan, Sumati, and... his father. Abhi snapped out of the trance, his eyes wide with shock. Bodies were dropping everywhere. Halls, Nina, and Tina were all racing down a flight of stairs—

Kraaaaboooom!

The stairs exploded, and Abhi lost his balance as they all crashed down. The smell of debris and blood filled the air. Someone was coughing. It was Halls. Abhi managed to rise.

"You okay, man?" Abhi said, helping him up.

"Yeah… I'm fine…" Halls said, staring at the metal rod protruding from his chest.

"Oh." Abhi cursed.

Quickly, they helped him up, dragging him to the side as firepower kept pouring down. Abhi's brows furrowed as he studied the position of the intruders. For all he knew, Leisha was still at his apartment, tied to a bomb.

"Hang in there…" Abhi said to Halls as he rose.

"No… stay…" Halls said, coughing blood. Nina and Tina had their heads bowed, tears streaming down their faces.

"You're gonna be fine, man… you're gonna be fine..." Abhi said, assessing the extent of the injury. Halls' ribcage was damaged, and his lungs were quickly filling with blood. He would die.

"Hang in there, man, just breathe… just… just breathe…" Abhi urged.

Halls chuckled. "I look taller, don't I?"

Abhi smiled, his eyes moist. "You do, man… you fucking do."

Halls' eyes were heavy now, bloodshot and teary. He grinned, squeezing Abhi's hand tightly.

"Take care of… my girls… for me, will ya?"

Abhi glared at Nina and Tina. His friend had an awkward way of handling people.

"I will, man… I will."

Halls brought his head close to Abhi's ear and whispered, "You're… you're still clean…"

Halls laughed, and Abhi could only smile. When he glanced at his friend again, he was met with a pair of lifeless eyes. Halls was dead.

"We should get going…" Nina said. Tina stayed behind.

* * *

January 3, 2020, Chicago (James's Lab)

James was racing down the stairs, Griss behind him.

"Hurry! Hurry!" A barrage of gunfire came at them.

"Where are we going?" James called as he rushed up another flight of stairs.

"You'll see soon enough," the old man replied.

"The girl… what about the girl?"

"Do you want to go and get her?" Griss said.

Finally, they reached the top of the stairs, a trapdoor hanging above their heads. It was sealed. Griss rushed forward, punching in a key code. The door swung open, ushering in a cool blue light. They rushed in.

The space was expansive. This was the top floor of the building, and the roof was airtight—perfectly sealed, with streams of blue light shooting from the corners of the room. James glanced at the heavy machine that occupied the center of the space.

"What in God's name is that?" His jaw dropped.

It was some sort of unmanned drone, retrofitted with seats so it could carry passengers if needed.

"What is that?"

James watched the entrance break open, and a sea of lights—each one different—began to ascend and descend in an aesthetically appealing pattern. Griss went over the details quickly until he stopped. This science discovery class was shortlived for both of them.

"Hello, hello," a man stood in the entrance of the aircraft. "It's a pleasure to meet you."

* * *

Stein received a phone call. They had found the girl, along with James Barnes and Griss, who had been on the missing person's list for the last 15 years, and a pleasant addition to the list of surprises.

"Any news about his brother… the other one?"

* * *

The wrecked van pulled up to a dilapidated building. Abhi and Nina jumped out of the car, racing toward what looked like an entrance. Nina stopped just short of it.

"What's wrong?"

"It's… it's been broken," she said, picking up the remains of a shattered padlock. Abhi ran a scan of the entire building.

"Come on, they're inside."

They both rushed in, walking through the ruins and dirt. There was no sign of life, at least not physically. Abhi could sense them. Their presence.

"Karan!" Abhi shouted.

Chapter 29

Karan, Sumati, and Gloria were in the warehouse after they were hit and picked up by Nina and Tina, without Hall's consent. Karan had, in the meantime, dreamt of the presence of his siblings and his father nearby, as well as where they were. Somehow, he felt his father was alive. He knew where he was and what had kept him away for twenty years. And now they had people trying to kill them. He had to get Sumati somewhere safe. Their assailants were coming for them.

"Is someone calling my name!" Karan said, hiding around the corner.

"It sounded like my brother…"

"What if they have him as a hostage?" Gloria said, peeking through a hole they had made. Somehow, they'd managed to break free from their plastic restraints and escaped the room they had been put in – but still within the same warehouse. They'd also covered their tracks, smearing the dusty floor to make sure no one could find them.

Sumati began coughing.

"Are you alright, Mom?" Karan felt his mother's pulse as she sat on the floor. Her eyes were exhausted, screaming of fatigue and prolonged dehydration.

"We'll be out of here soon… ok, hang on, hang on…"

Footsteps were getting closer.

"Karan!"

Karan's gaze shot to Gloria.

"It's not what you think, Karan. I'm sure of it," she said. She steadied herself and gestured that they needed to keep moving. Karan carried Sumati on his back. She was sobbing now.

The footsteps were louder now, getting closer. Gloria and Karan, with his mother on his back, broke into a run. Karan kept hearing his name. This was all wrong, he thought. Something in his head kept screaming that this was wrong. He had seen this all happening in a dream, the last night. Something was going to happen here—someone was going to die. His heart raced.

"Stop!" Karan said to Gloria.

"What are you doing?" she said, watching him set his mother down.

"I've seen this before..."

"Not now, Karan. Come on."

"I'm serious, someone dies here. We've got to stop..."

"Now's not the time, Karan. You're jeopardizing our lives!"

"I've seen this in a dream!"

At that moment, Gloria swung her gun forward. It whizzed past Karan and hit a figure she had spotted in the dark. The gun struck Nina on the throat. In a flash, Gloria pounced on her, landing blows and kicks.

Karan watched the two women, then saw a figure ahead in the shadows. He reached for Gloria's gun.

"Stay back!"

"Karan, it's me—it's me—"

"Shoot her, Karan! Don't freaking listen to her!" Gloria yelled, trying to wrestle the gun from Karan.

"Don't do this..." Karan said.

Suddenly, a sharp shriek pierced the air. Gloria rose, panting, and shot the woman.

"No..." The voice in the shadows leaped forward to save the girl, but the bullet grazed past him, causing a massive bleed. It stuck Nina close to her heart. She dropped to the floor with her eyes open looking at the sky.

The woman staggered forward, bits of warehouse light illuminating her face. And then they saw the person, who was trying to save the woman. It was…

Abhi.

"Abhi!"

* * *

Karan fell to his knees, crouched beside his brother as Abhi continued bleeding. Abhi's gaze was fixed on Nina's lifeless body. He was saying something.

"He said… to protect her…"

"Hold on, bro… hold on…"

"Halls said to protect her…"

Those were the last words Abhi spoke before passing out.

"Borda was killed by one of these twins, or perhaps both. We should have taken them out earlier," Gloria reasoned, justifying her action, and the job she was recruited for.

Moments later, sirens filled the air. Leisha leapt out of her vehicle when she saw Abhi lying still. Tina joined her upon seeing her sister.

Leisha checked Abhi's pulse. It was weak, but he was alive. Very much alive. She glared at the other sister, Tina, who was perched over her sister's body, mourning. Gloria looked that way too, thinking of ways to get rid of the twin. She couldn't.

Sumati rose from where she sat when she saw someone from afar.

"My… my baby…" Sumati cried, throwing her arms around Chandra. Someone from Stein's team had brought her in, before she left on Griss's unmanned aircraft.

"My goodness, Mom… I've… I've missed you…"

Chandra's eyes darted towards the men carrying a stretcher for the wounded.

"What happened to Abhi?" Chandra was weeping. Just then, Stein joined them, asking to see Karan.

"I'm sorry to interrupt the family time..." Stein said, clearing his throat.

"It's okay..."

"We... I... owe you, Karan. A lot..." Stein said, removing his shades. "Gloria told me everything... I wanted to personally thank you for... everything."

"It's alright, Stein. She's a great officer."

"Karan, there's something we found back at the lab... something we believe might be of interest to your family."

Chapter 30

January 4, 2020, Highland Park Hospital

The hospital was well-lit when Abhi woke up, the intense light causing a mental strain. His chest hurt like hell. He remembered what it felt like when his father disappeared. Regret filled his heart. Regret for what he hadn't done. He should've hugged his dad right there, back in Calcutta, before Dad left. A conversation that never ended.

"Hey there…" he looked around, his face collapsing into a smile. "Chandra…"

He tried to get up, but he couldn't.

"Hey, slow down. You're only just recovering."

"Recovery has been a long process?" Abhi smirked, causing Chandra to nudge him on his leg.

"Ouch!" Abhi coughed. "That… that hurt…?"

"A lot?"

"You can't imagine", imitating Karan.

"I'm… I'm sorry…" Chandra massaged the spot, causing Abhi to squint, one eye open, as a mischievous grin spread across his face.

"Yeah, that feels better."

"There's someone who wants to see you…" Chandra said, her gaze motioning to the door. Abhi followed her gaze. Standing in the doorway was Leisha.

* * *

Leisha sat next to him long after Chandra excused herself.

"How are you holding up?" Abhi asked. He blinked.

"They say you'll be out in a month..." Leisha said, her gaze fixed on his face.

"Yeah, that's terrible..."

"What's the first thing you'll do when you're out?"

"I don't know... some peaceful place, let my head float... I think the cops will arrest me the same day."

"I think you are not a fugitive, anymore."

Leisha produced a file she had brought with her and held it out for Abhi.

"Tina confessed to the murder of Borda?"

"What?"

"Yes... that can't happen. I'm supposed to take care of her..."

"And you will. There's evidence she has a brain disorder. Three federally approved psychiatrists confirmed this. She'll spend a few years behind bars, and if she's good, she'll get early parole. You will be a good son-in-law to Halls?"

Abhi inhaled. Looked at Leisha and smiled.

"You haven't answered."

"What?" Abhi said.

"What would you do when you're out of here?"

"I don't know, maybe I'll—"

She kissed him.

Right then, Karan walked in on them.

"Oops, sorry." He rolled back, shutting the door and went back to his call.

Leisha's cheeks turned red immediately.

"I'm... I'm sorry," she said nervously. Abhi just stared back, blinking. That was unexpected. A complacent grin spread across Abhi's lips.

He kissed her back.

* * *

Karan had been at the hospital since the incident, waiting for updates on his brother. Sumati and Chandra had gone home,.

He had left several messages for Priya, but she hadn't reached out. They hadn't spoken since the day he left for Legacy Inc. building

Strange.

"Good to catch you here , Karan," Stein said as he walked in, with Gloria right behind him. Gloria had a formal dress on and Karan couldn't take his eyes off her.They had just entered the hospital lobby.

"James Barnes will be charged with murder and unlawful detention…"

"I'm sorry," Karan interrupted while pointing to his cell phone, "Was multitasking – will you please repeat the last part?"

"Sure I can do that. Barnes goes in for illegal experiments on humans under the pretext of extending scientific knowledge," Gloria explained.

"Barnes should be spending a good portion of his life behind bars," Stein said. "His accomplice, however…"

"He had an accomplice?" Karan raised an eyebrow.

"As a matter of fact, yes. A.G. Griss. He's more like a godfather. He created the extraction market and is the man, who owns the trust that owns Legacy Inc. We gather that he has another facility in the Philippines. No leads on that yet. He also has a network of accomplices who are yet to be identified."

Karan shrugged. "I don't understand when did they change their course – as they had a good cause when they started. On well, you can't speak for everyone."

"That's right. Well, Griss will be having a hard time serving his life sentence."

Karan nodded, watching Stein's consistently appalling attempt at humor.

"For the fraudulence matter at hand, we've finalized discussions with our 'friends in high places' regarding your company..."

Karan straightened up, leaning back. "And?"

"The board is willing to grant you an exception."

"By 'exception,' you mean lifting the litigation, unfreezing my company, that sort of thing?"

"Yes, something like that."

"Alright, I'm listening."

"So, you're being offered a condition, Karan."

Karan read on. "All the proposed structural changes are to be carried out only if Mr. Karan Roy agrees to take into your custody item 7-2B-6."

"What's that?" Karan said, keeping the file on the coffee table.

"Back at the warehouse, I told you there was something you'd want to see."

Karan nodded.

"Follow me."

They strolled out of the hospital, and drove in the car and stopped in front of a posh downtown hotel. They took the elevator. The elevator descended rapidly, reaching an underground facility. As they exited, Karan wondered just how many underground facilities he had been in that week.

"This way, please," Gloria led the way. Karan followed, with Stein right next to him.

At the push of a button, a door swung open. Karan saw a fog filled giant glass room, large enough to house two Mercedes side by side.

But Stein didn't stop. "When our boys raided Barnes and Griss's place, they found your sister. She said she knew something. She led them deep into this basement. And there, they found this glass room."

Karan had no idea what he was talking about. He leaned closer, his hand brushing against the glass. Inside was mist. Slowly, the mist began to clear as they opened the glass door. Karan squinted, focusing on something that resembled a face and make sense of it. As the mist dissipated, Karan's hands slipped from the glass wall, his eyes shaking as he slowly turned to Stein.

What in God's name?

Seated in a chair, staring blankly at a wall, was an elderly Abhi—no, it was Anurag Roy. Anurag didn't seem to be moving that much.

* * *

As Karan drove back to the Hospital, his mind wandered to his conversation with Stein.

"Your father has been kept here since the first extraction failure. He had threatened to expose them for their work. They couldn't kill him, as they required samples from him to explore other possibilities for extraction... and he was a highly valuable asset, considering his psychic abilities. So, they built him his own home in this hotel basement. This hotel is also owned by Legacy, Inc."

His mind also flashed further back to the other major update he'd gotten from Stein.

"Someone has been working for Barnes and Griss's competition, someone who knows a lot about you guys," Stein had explained.

"Our records show a stream of encoded emails flowing from your IP address to an undetermined location in the Atlantic. Are you aware of this?"

"Not at all," Karan had said, nervously.

"We were able to decode most of these conversations. It appears the person in question works for a different organization with an interest quite similar to Griss and Barnes'."

"The person in question, we believe, had the intent to pass secrets about your family…" Stein had continued. "You, Karan, and your family of specials are among the rarest breeds of humans with such profound gifts… and you are highly prized. They will stop at nothing to get you. But we have a better plan…"

Karan waited for it.

"We will strike first."

Karan nodded, shifting in his chair. He cleared his throat. "We?"

Is today the day when all truths have to come out? He had leaned back, still staring at Gloria and listening to Stein.

"We have one final favor to ask, Karan. We want to visit your home with you…"

Karan went with Stein and Gloria. They got off the elevator and made a sharp left turn, avoiding the CCTV cameras.

Karan opened the main door.

Just as I thought.

As Karan walked in, he was greeted with a familiar smell. It was the same scent he had been greeted with all these years waking up at his apartment. Sweet and sour yet memorable.

His mind rushed back to the last time he was at his apartment, just before this detour. It was very quiet. Everywhere.

There was no sign of his fiancée. She hadn't been home in days. Dishes filled the sink, scattered clothes lay around… everything in chaos. He found that some of his files were missing:

birth certificate, blood tests, clothes, hairbrush. Most of his personal effects were gone.

An empty home.

however, as he got closer to the bathroom, he noticed the white noise of the shower. Someone was in the shower. There was messy bed around the corner, with a few bags strewn across the mattress.

Someone has been packing!

Strangely, Karan was drawn to a low table. He reached it, noticing shortened cigarettes and ashes scattered atop it. Underneath the ash was a photo. He picked up a rumpled photo. It was a group photo. He noticed it had his father and a couple other people, all drinking beer under a Happy New Millenium sign. Just then, the bathroom door swung open, and a woman draped in a towel stepped out. She stopped when she spotted she had company. Karan glared at her, a calm grin spreading across his face.

"Hello, Priya."

Chapter 31

Couple of weeks later

Abhi stood on both legs, his thighs crushing with pain. He took the first step. Pain. He took the next. More pain. Soon, he took some more, and the pain seemed to double. He wanted to stop, to swear through his teeth. But he couldn't. He found that he couldn't stop; that he didn't want to stop. It became pleasurable. The pain.

Leisha glared at him. "I told you."

Abhi grinned in the pair of crocs he was wearing. They looked deliciously ugly, yet they had an awkward appeal to him.

"You mentioned it," Abhi said, reclining into the chair as the wind of the beach blew his hat away. Chandra giggled next to him. She was next to him, in a wheelchair with really fat tires—fat enough to let it run on the beach soil. Sumati was perched beside her.

Abhi watched Chandra and Leisha giggle. Too bad Priya wasn't here with them. A few days back, Karan had confirmed Priya's involvement.

Priya worked for Ajit—and Ajit planted her with Karan to get information on Karan's brain patterns. Bhavna, Ajit's daughter was not aware nor involved at all in this. Priya had also been spying on the family this whole time.

Abhi had found it hard to believe, as he felt strongly that she was deeply in love with Karan. Karan had said he would look for ways to have them reduce her sentence.

Abhi watched the waves of Lake Michigan play around, his lips arching. Finally, they got the lowdown on their father's disappearance.

Anurag Roy had been kidnapped on December 31st, 1999. While his abductors had tried to extract his abilities with limited success, he had practiced prolonged out-of-body meditation. That prevented extraction. During that time, he helped his children unlock their abilities and guided them out of harm's way. Now, their father was at a health center, undergoing therapy.

In talking to other spiritual leaders in Tarapeeth, the family found that during an Amavasya Puja ceremony, Anurag had felt dizzy—as if a meteorite had struck him. Shortly thereafter he realized he had special powers and he could get out-of-body.

Abhi grinned. He had kept wondering who had been calling him from a private line—he had stayed up all night thinking about the possibilities. It was Anurag Roy himself who had been leaving recorded messages. Who would believe that?

Abhi was reading Ross' journal out loud: "Lewis and Luke intercepted Dad at the airport. Lewis, who was a friend of James, knew from one Ajit that Anurag was flying in. Ajit was trying to develop an investment management system using parapsychological remote viewing and wanted Dad's help in making a model that could predict the prices of stocks and financial instruments.

They failed, which is why he started working on pharmaceutical exports. Ajit and James had jointly borrowed money from Halls, for this venture, but instead, they got him to prison, and also got Anurag embroiled in that case. Due to that, and the fact that Ajit couldn't pay back in time, his son, Borda, was killed. James took Griss's help to get Halls his money. They started the extraction business to do so – again taking advantage of the initial work done by Anurag and making him the guinea pig as well, in the advancements. AG Griss, by the way, could've been a stock market genius or a market maker with his product ideas, but instead he chose to get into this evil business. Also, brothers Lewis and Luke were helping James with new finds to further the extraction market—this is where Pierre met with an accident, while saving Chandra. It was Luke who pushed him to the street. Borda wanted to get some secretive matter to blackmail James mixed with the paperwork I was going to collect, but James found out from Lewis and somehow tried pulling the plug by informing his henchmen to take me out in India. I unknowingly teleported and saved myself. And the rest, we'll uncover soon."

Abhi inhaled, content that the family was safe by the water. Also, their father was undergoing rehabilitation therapy and they were told that he will recover fully within the next few months.

* * *

"I'd like to get on those, Mom." Chandra pointed to a Ferris wheel. Sumati shook her head vigorously.

"Pleaaaase." Chandra pleaded.

"There's no way you're climbing that thing."

Chandra finally pulled her close and whispered in her ear. Soon, Sumati was up, guiding Chandra towards the Ferris wheel.

"Now you two, have a great time, okay?" Sumati said. Abhi shot her a cursory glance. Chandra was giggling.

When they were gone, Leisha leaned forward.

"What was that about?"

Abhi chuckled. "I don't think you'd want to know."

"What if I do?"

Abhi grinned nervously as Leisha's nonchalant words hung in the air.

He kissed her. "So, let us start from the beginning. We never got a chance to introduce ourselves much and our first few dates were spent in keeping ourselves alive…what do you think life is?"

Abhi watched his mother leave, slightly embarrassed. But Leisha drew his face to hers and kissed him hard. They didn't stop there.

Karan stepped in. "Sorry guys—running late. Spoke with Tina over the phone – apparently the fake diamonds that Ross had spoken to Owens about were meth crystals and worth as much as diamonds – even more. Borda knew about that. It is gone now. Somebody has them."

Just then, Karan's phone rang.

Bhavna called Karan and listened to everything about her father, Ajit and about Priya. Bhavna expressed her disappointment about Priya, who worked for her father. She also didn't know that Priya and Karan were seeing each other.

Bhavna also revealed something about her father, Ajit, that kept Karan's jaw open.

Acknowledgements

First of all, I want to express my sincere gratitude to you, the reader, for taking the time to read my book. Your curiosity means the world to me. I would also like to extend my heartfelt thanks to the creators of books, movies, and TV series around the world that delve into the realm of parapsychological thrillers. Your groundbreaking work has laid the foundation for my own exploration of these fascinating subjects.

In particular, I am deeply appreciative of the emerging body of work that explores the power of the mind, spirituality, lucid dreaming, and out-of-body experiences. These areas have captured my imagination and provided valuable insight into the depths of human potential. The challenges and successes in the lives of non immigrant visa holders and those, who were part of the Y2K exodus are now being more widely addressed in contemporary literature. This shift in perspective has been crucial in shaping my own narrative. Additionally, the profound societal changes brought about by the COVID-19 pandemic have revolutionized not just how we work and socialize, but how we think and perceive the world around us. As a result, my work blends true data with a generous dose of fiction, seeking to weave together all these threads into a compelling story.

The most significant and heartfelt acknowledgment goes to my family, whose unwavering support and encouragement have been the driving force behind this book. My wonderful wife, Aindrila Gupta, has been the true inspiration behind my interest in parapsychology. The character of Chandra is a direct reflection of her influence, as she is the one who developed the character for the book. And for that, I am eternally grateful. My daughters, Naija Niyogi and Maya Niyogi, have also played an important role in shaping this book. Their inquisitive nature and thought-provoking questions about the chapters in progress have kept me grounded and made me rethink my assumptions along the way.

I am also deeply thankful to my father, Sumanta Niyogi, whose wisdom, knowledge, and constant encouragement have been a source of inspiration throughout my life and career. My late mother, Sandhya Niyogi, whose stories and nurturing spirit shaped much of who I am today, will forever hold a special place in my heart.

A special mention goes to Suhail Mathur of the Book Bakers Literary Agency, whose belief in my work and expert guidance were instrumental in helping me secure a contract with Om Books. As an award-winning author, Suhail's empathy and insightful recommendations helped me refine my work and align it with the greater literary landscape.

My heartfelt thanks also go to Shantanu Ray Chaudhuri (Shantanu Da) of Om Books, who not only provided a home for my fiction but also played a key role in meticulously planning the launch of this book. His dedication and vision have been invaluable. I would also like to extend my sincere appreciation to Saba Umme Salma, whose exceptional copy-editing skills and collaborative spirit helped bring my story to life, making it adaptable not only for sequels but also for potential film and television adaptations . Finally, I wish to express my sincere gratitude to Anirban Bhattacharyya and Sagarika Chakraborty for their insightful feedback and steadfast support throughout the process, which significantly contributed to enhancing the cinematic quality, relatability, and emotional resonance of the work.